I0739203

Aiki Flinthart

Sold!

Aiki Flinthart

ISBN-13: 978-0-9945660-0-3
Computing Advantages & Training P/L

Chapter One

"You did *what?!*" Kali swung herself upright on the couch, bare feet hitting the floor with a slap.

She shivered and tucked her feet back up under her jeans-clad legs as the cool wood chilled her toes. A cold breeze snuck down the collar of her jumper. She pulled it tight against her neck. A newer house would be nice; one without draughts, possums and spiders.

Her feckless brother sniggered, helping himself to a beer from her fridge.

"You heard me." He peered further into the fridge, seemingly oblivious to her infuriated squeaks. "Do you have anything to eat that isn't a vegetable? Honestly," he glanced over his shoulder, green eyes sparkling at his incensed twin, "how does the daughter of a cattle farmer become a vegetarian?"

"I'm not a vegetarian, I just eat healthy - unlike some people I know. Stop trying to change the subject!" She jumped up and paced around the small room, waving her hands for emphasis. She'd never been one to sit still for long and found her brother's laissez-faire attitude annoying. "Castor James Brooker you can't just *do* something like that to me! It's...it's... illegal. It has to be."

Castor mimicked her. "Kalisa Jane Brooker I can, I did, it's done. Not illegal. I checked. Suffer, kiddo." He picked up an apple, inspected it and elbowed shut the fridge door. "Anyway, how else were you going to get there?"

She flung up her hands in despair and continued pacing. "I would've found some way. I'm resourceful. I've got a whole day to work it out. I'd've thought of something."

Her unrepentant brother sank onto the couch, beer in hand. He put sock-clad feet up on the coffee table, long legs outstretched in stylish casual cream trousers.

"Too late. You're the organised one, you've had three months to think of something, but you didn't. If I didn't know how close you and Amy are I'd suspect you didn't really want to go. You'd regret it forever if you missed this, so I got it sorted for you. Stop complaining. You pay nothing, you get to the island and you have your plus one for the wedding as well."

"But...but," she sputtered, shoving back a strand of long, black hair. "Caz, I can't just get on a plane with some complete stranger! Who knows where he might take me."

Castor flicked the TV to a football match. "He'll have to file a flight plan and you can take a GPS locator."

"Oh!" Kali reached around behind the TV and yanked the cord out, brandishing it at her brother. "It's not that simple. You put me on Ebay for God's sake. You *have* to cancel the transaction. You *can't* sell a person on Ebay!"

"Chill." He yawned. "I didn't sell *you*, just the right to take you to Amy's wedding tomorrow. She's your best friend and you were stuck. Now you aren't. You should be thanking me, not yelling at me and interrupting the football. Now plug the TV back in or I'll leave."

She put her hands on her hips, glaring at him. "Hardly a threat."

She held the cord between two fingers and deliberately let it drop on the floor. Outside, a parrot scrawked an echo of her annoyance. A lawnmower growled to life. Friday morning went on around them.

He quirked an eyebrow at her. "You really want me to leave without telling you who won the auction and how much he paid?"

"What do you mean 'won'?" Her heart plummeted. "You told me the auction wasn't finished. You said there was another three hours."

"I lied. I do that. You should know me by now." He chuckled. "Three day auction. Finished last night."

She groaned and sank back onto the couch. "You can*not* be serious." She pinched the bridge of her nose. "You've honestly sold me to some desperate prat on Ebay?"

"Not sure I'd class him as a prat, per se." He took a swig of beer. "In fact, I'm certain I wouldn't. Nice guy, actually."

The leather couch creaked as he got up, plugged the TV in and sat back with a sigh of relief. The football blared to life.

Snatching the remote she muted the sound, determined to have it out with him. "Oh, come on. What sort of man is desperate enough to buy time with a girl on an ebay auction? What sort of man is even *searching* for something like that on Ebay?"

"Hey, I *am* in marketing, remember," Castor reminded her. "I didn't just throw you on and leave it to chance. You were well-advertised in select circles, believe me."

"That's ridiculous, disgusting and it makes you sound like a pimp," Kali said. "Who would pay just to fly me somewhere? It's not like I'm super model material or anything. Wait!" She gaped at her brother in horrified disgust. "You'd better not have offered them anything else!"

He threw back his head and laughed, then regarded her with something like compassion. "Don't stress. All strictly above-board. As for 'not super-model material', when was the last time you checked in the mirror, kiddo."

The cushion made a handy weapon. She whacked him with it. "When I looked at you, twin bro. Black hair. Green eyes. Except you need to get out in the sun more. You're becoming a bit vampirish. I do like that colour shirt on you, though." She pointed at his forest-green polo.

Snorting, her brother picked up another cushion and hit her back. "If I had your face, and I was a girl, I sure as hell wouldn't be single. Beats me why you still are, actually." He measured her from beneath his brows.

She returned his cynicism with level disdain. He knew exactly why she was still single. She opened her mouth to say so but he held up a hand.

"Your problem is that you don't know how to make the most of what you've got. Do you even *own* a mirror?"

She sneered at her handsome brother. "Of course I do, and I do know how to dress and wear makeup, I just don't care and you know why. I don't need to glam up. I'm good enough as I am."

Castor made a sound of frustration and switched the sound back on. "Agreed; you are, Kali, but there's a difference between not caring and deliberately downplaying. You aren't who you were six years ago. Move on or you're still letting him run your life."

A little hurt, she sat on the coffee table in front of him, blocking the TV. He tried to peer around her. She swayed sideways.

"I'm not blind or stupid. I know I'm pretty, it's just not important. If the only reason someone wants me is because of how I look...well, I'd rather not go there again." She grimaced, fiddling with a lock of her hair. "Anyway. You're changing the subject again. Who won the auction? Hey," she sat up straight, "I know - I can just refund him the money and it will be all over."

He took a swallow of his beer, raising it to her in a

toast. "Sorry, he already donated it to your favourite charity, as per the auction instructions. Yes! Goal!" He punched the air, peering around her at the box.

"What!?" She gulped, lightheaded. "You mean I don't even get the money? How is that fair?"

He smirked at her. "You're the one who's always telling mum and dad how well you're doing; how you don't need their help. You don't need the money."

A punch in the arm did little but make him laugh

"Shut up, Caz. I *am* fine. It's just harder to start up my own business than I thought. I could've used an extra couple dollars at the moment - especially if I have to be away for nine days at this wedding. Damn." She chewed on her lip and glared at her irritating brother. "So why did you donate it to charity?"

He quirked that knowing little half-smile he knew annoyed her so much. "Partly because now you can't back out on the deal; partly because I knew that if you *had* the money in your hot little hand, you'd have trouble giving it back it if you did want to back out."

"Oh come on." She curled a lip at him. "How hard could it be to give back? I'll pay him out of my own pocket, then. The auction couldn't have finished for more than a hundred, max, in that short a time."

He considered her, clearly amused. The roar of the tv crowd punctuated the silence.

"More?" She frowned, unbelieving.

He leered and waggled his eyebrows, green eyes glittering with unholy delight.

She blinked at him, heart sinking. Much more and she wouldn't be able to repay the winner. She'd be stuck with him, whoever he was. "How much more?"

Castor intertwined his hands behind his head and leaned back, watching her from under drooping lids. "Quite a lot, actually. Even I was surprised and I quite like you - when you're being nice to me." His attention drifted back to the television.

"Thanks for that ringing endorsement." She grabbed at his arm to pull him away from the game. "OK, you'd better tell me how much then."

"Try three hundred and fifty seven," he replied coolly.

With a small spurt of something suspiciously like hurt feelings, Kali slumped. "Oh, that's not so bad. I can repay him that and still have enough to pay the rent. I'll just-"

"Thousand," he finished, expression sly.

The room shrank. She stilled, her heart pounding in her ears. "I'm sorry?"

"Three hundred and fifty-seven *thousand*," her brother repeated, chortling. "Five bidders. A hundred and eighty bids in total. Three hundred and fifty-seven thousand dollars donated to the Cancer fund in your name. I think they're going to send you a plaque."

She opened her mouth, but nothing came out. A strange roaring sound filled her ears. She held on tighter to the coffee table, lest the tilting of the world tip her onto the floor. She lifted her face toward the high wooden ceiling, for once barely seeing the cobwebs lurking in the shadows there. Then she stared out the wide windows, not admiring the brilliant blue spring sky over Brisbane, nor the eye-watering, purple jacaranda tree blooming in her back yard.

Her voice came back, albeit a little croaky. "Are you serious?"

Something in her tone must have caught Castor's attention. He blinked at her with mild concern. "Sure. It's all above board. Three fifty-seven large. All paid for already. What's wrong?"

"Surely, Castor," she said severely, blood rushing back to her head, carried by anger and disbelief, "even your flighty brain can get the concept of slavery. I mean, what is this guy going to expect for that kind of money?" She pushed back her hair with shaking hands, trying to find the words to convince him how bad an idea this was.

He'd always been impulsive and headstrong, although he'd settled somewhat in the last couple of years, but this reached beyond even his normal level of insanity.

"Can't you see how scary a position you've put me in? I'll be alone with some complete stranger on a two hour plane flight to a private island. What if he's a serial killer?"

Her brother relaxed. "Kali-baby, you're just going to have to trust me on this. He's no serial killer and you're in safe hands." He sent her another smug smirk. "He's a well-respected businessman from here in Brisbane. He has a Lear jet. You'll be there in an hour or so, max. It's pretty hard to murder someone on a small plane and not get noticed."

"Oh!" She picked up the cushion again and threw it at him. He deflected it with leisurely ease, barely even distracted from the screen. "I won't go. You can't make me get on a plane with someone I've never met. Not even for Amy. She can do without a bridesmaid. It's not my fault I couldn't go with the rest of the bridal party yesterday. For chrissake!" She dropped her head into her hands. "Who has a wedding on a private island accessible only by private plane anyway?"

Her brother patted her shoulder. "Someone who can afford it. Amy's famous and Max is super-rich, remember? They're trying to avoid the media."

He squeezed her shoulder and turned serious just for a moment. "Trust me Kali, it's ok. You'll just have to believe that I've done this for a very good reason and you will be perfectly safe."

She eyed him doubtfully. "What reason?"

He grinned, the brief solemnity falling away. "Just have a little faith. It's important and it's ok, I promise. Besides, if you want to be there for Amy, you've run out of options. Either take this one or don't go."

Kali groaned. "I have to go, you know that you pig. I

owe Amy. Besides, she's my best friend and I promised to wear that stupid pink dress she picked out. Pink! On me. Hey," she punched his arm again, "stop changing the subject. Dammit! I trust *you,* but you've put me in the most freakingly uncomfortable position. It had better be earth-shatteringly important."

"Ow! It is. Sorry." He grinned without a hint of apology. "It's going to get worse in..ow.. about..." he checked his watch, "fifteen minutes."

"What? Why?" She stopped in mid-punch, horrified. "What now? Have you told Mum and Dad or something?"

"Nah," he waved away the possibility, "I figured you might be a little put off by the idea of getting into a plane with a stranger."

"Y'think?"

"So," he ignored the interruption and took a mouthful of beer, "I invited him to come over for lunch today. You can get to know him before you leave tomorrow. I'll even stay and chaperone."

For a moment, Kali could only gape at her brother, rendered speechless by his audacity. He ignored her some more, cheering another goal by his favourite team.

"I don't have any lunch-food in the fridge," she tried, desperate, "and I have an appointment in an hour."

Castor flicked her a quick, ironic look and pulled his phone out of his pocket. Before she could speak again, he'd called her local Indian restaurant, ordered three serves of butter chicken, then sent a text and tucked his phone away again.

Clearly talking him out of this was an exercise in futility. She shut her mouth with a snap. Leaning her chin on her hands, she rested her elbows on her knees and studied the polished wood floorboards for a few minutes. What to do?

She did trust Castor's judgment and wasn't all that concerned with being alone with a stranger. She was reasonably confident she could deal with any unwanted advances. Castor obviously had some agenda here he wasn't sharing, which was annoying, but not alarming. He'd never put her in any sort of real danger.

The biggest issue was Castor's unceasing attempts to butt into her life and rearrange it. He seemed to think being her twin gave him some sort of right to 'fix' whatever section of her life he thought needed it. This clearly wasn't just a helpful way of getting her to her best friend's wedding. Castor was messing with her love life – about six years too late, though. Obviously he still felt guilty about not being around when she'd needed him and thought he could make up for it by, what, pimping her out like this? He was mad.

OK, well if that's how he wanted it, two could play at that game. She smirked to herself and left the lounge room without another word. Castor lifted his beer in salute as she walked past.

"That's a girl, go get dressed up. Make an impression."

She punched him in the arm again as she exited the room. He blew her a kiss.

Fifteen minutes later, a knock on the front door echoed through the old house. She hurried to put the final touches to her outfit. After a second knock, laconic footsteps and male voices said Castor had got off his butt and answered the door. Her bedroom lay right at the back of the house, so she couldn't hear distinct words, just murmurs and laughter. She surveyed her reflection in the mirror. Laughing at her, were they? Well, let's see what Mr Ebay thought when he saw what he'd bought. Satisfied with her work, she twitched the plaid flannel shirt into place, jammed on her hat and yanked the door open. Hooking her thumbs through the belt loops of her jeans, she strode out into the living room, switching to a swagger just as the two men inside turned at the sound of her booted footsteps.

A first glimpse of him made her pause. Had she chosen the right tactic? The man standing next to Castor was, not to put too fine a point on it, hot. Really hot. Smoking freaking amazingly hot. Just over six foot, with dark blond, short, artfully messy hair; eyes of the most amazing storm-grey, full of secrets, intelligence and humour; and a half-smile that made her stomach quiver. It wasn't just his looks though: he exuded quiet confidence and moved with the lithe power of someone in total control of their body; not just a gym-junkie but a man who used his body for more than sitting around boardrooms; an athlete of sorts.

If she wasn't so mad with Castor and, by association, with this guy, she'd be tempted to bolt back into her room and change. It was too late for that, though and, since she was still pissed off with Castor, she would carry on. At least it would send the message that this guy needed to keep his hands to himself. She was *not* waiting for some man to disrupt her carefully reconstructed life.

Besides, she made it a point, these days, never to dress to impress men. Being pretty for men was not the reason for her existence. Nor was doing what men told her to do, as Castor was about to learn.

"Oh for God's sake." Castor ran fingers through his dark hair at the sight of her. "Seriously?"

The stranger glanced quickly between brother and sister, obviously wondering what the issue was.

She put on her best, broadest okker outback Australian accent and stuck out a hand.

"G'day mate. I'm Kali." She pretended to chew gum, enjoying the groan from her irritating brother.

"Alex Schiffer." Her date took her hand in his and shook it with exactly the right amount of strength. "Nice to meet you."

"Too right!" she returned. "Nice to meet a decent city bloke like you. Right up my alley, Caz." She elbowed

Castor. "Good one bro. Bloody beaut! Let's go get some grub."

She tipped her Akubra hat back on her head, jammed her thumbs back in the belt-loops of her jeans and stuck one booted foot out.

Alex swept her cowgirl outfit from toe to head, with just a hint of devilish humour lurking in his eyes; as though he knew some private joke at her expense.

"No need to go out. I picked up the Indian on the way past." He gestured at two plastic bags on the cheap pine dining table. "Wasn't sure you'd be…dressed…to go out."

Castor snorted a laugh and handed him a beer.

Momentarily thrown off-stride, Kali glared at both of them, mumbled something about getting plates and bolted for the kitchen. He hadn't batted an eyelid.

As she passed her brother, he reached over and tweaked one of her ridiculous braids, dragging her head close and murmuring in her ear, "Unnecessary, idiot. I've known Alex for seven years. He's a friend."

After lunch, she leaned back in the lounge seat, arms and legs folded, eyeing her date with deep suspicion. Opposite, Alex Schiffer relaxed into an armchair, his long legs stretched out comfortably and one arm laid out across the back of the seat. He wore long black pants and a grey polo shirt that matched his eyes. Not quite business attire but not weekend-casual either. Expensive, well-made clothing in which he appeared utterly at ease.

Castor bore the burden of what conversation struggled around the table as he bolted his food. Then, apparently satisfied he'd done his duty in every way and with a nasty wink for Kali, he'd practically run out the door, leaving the pair in awkward silence. Well, awkward for her. As far as she could tell Alex was perfectly comfortable with the whole situation. He took a sip from his beer, saying nothing, evidently waiting for her to initiate conversation.

Unable to stand the silence any longer, she blurted out

the first thing that came to mind.

"So, Caz tells me you own your own business. It's Friday, why aren't you working?"

Alex's beautifully-sculpted mouth twitched into a half-smile, tolerant humour flashing for a moment. "I could ask you the same question but I won't because it would sound rude. I'm here because I wanted to see who I'd bought."

Chapter Two

Jaw dropping, Kali clutched at the armrest in an effort to restrain herself from punching him in the nose. Honestly. Who he'd *bought?*   The flicker of a wicked gleam in his eye stopped her short. Gritting her teeth, she kept a lid on her automatic reaction. He was deliberately pushing buttons to get a response. Why?

Alex leaned forward suddenly. She threw up a hand in automatic defence and leaned away, alarmed. He put his beer down on the coffee table. Reaching into a back pocket he pulled out a black leather wallet, selected a card of some sort and held it up between two fingers before flicking it onto the coffee table. It slid to a halt in front of her.

Embarrassed, she pressed her lips together. She picked it up. His driver's licence. She inspected it closely. Counterfeiting these things was easy if you knew how. It seemed in order. The photo was surprisingly good; his address in an expensive part of Brisbane. He could apparently drive not only a car but a motorbike and a boat as well. Of course.

"So what's with the cowgirl costume?" He regarded her over the rim of his beer bottle. "Trying to discourage me?"

"What do you mean?" She lifted her brows superciliously. "This is how I always dress. Like it or lump it."

He said nothing. He didn't seem to be a big talker. He simply took out his phone, tapped at it for a few seconds then reversed it toward her. There, on the screen, was a full-body glam shot of her, next to the final payout figure on Ebay. She groaned. It was a shot a photographer friend of hers had snapped as part of a photographic exhibit two years before. Sepia-toned and tasteful, her back was to the camera. The only colour was the green of her smoky, sultry eyes. It had had taken the makeup artist an hour to get the makeup right. Unfortunately, even though nothing important was visible, it was still obvious she was naked.

Now the 'not dressed to go out' remark from before made total sense.

"I'm going to *kill* him!" Her cheeks burned.

"I don't see why." Alex examined the photo. "It's a great photo. Very artistic."

"Yes, but seeing that, any guy would…" she floundered at the polite, blank inquiring look from him, "would...think that...I mean…wouldn't they?" She ground to a halt as a new thought took hold. How to ask politely, though?

"Well," he interrupted before she could frame the question uppermost in her mind. Unfolding from the chair he reclaimed his licence and tucked it into his wallet before finishing his sentence. "Thankyou for lunch. I'll send a car for you tomorrow morning around eight, shall I?"

Kali blinked at him, derailed. For a relaxed seeming guy he was very decisive and very annoying. She firmly pushed aside the small voice in her head telling her how much she liked decisive men. A fine line existed between decisive and controlling and she'd experienced too much of the latter to take a risk.

She followed him to the front door, ambiguous about the whole situation. This short lunch left her feeling unqualified to judge him as a person. On the one hand, he seemed ok and Castor vouched for him. Plus, she did need a lift to the wedding island and a date for the wedding and reception. There was no doubt Alex Schiffer was eye-candy and a small, very female part of her itched to see the reactions from Amy's Hollywood glam friends' when nobody Kalisa Brooker walked in with him on her arm.

On the other hand, the big mystery remained: why had he bid such an outrageous price for the privilege of flying a girl he'd never met to a wedding full of people he didn't know?

Their footsteps echoed hollowly on the creaking floorboards. At the end of the hall, Alex opened the door and spun back, his eyes still holding that enigmatic hint of humour and secrets she found both irritating and intriguing. He held out a hand. She shook it. They stood, just considering each other, for several moments; Kali trying hard to ignore the warmth and strength of his hand, him apparently unmoved.

Unable to help herself, she tilted her head to one side and asked the first of two questions bugging her.

"Why did you bid for me, Mr Schiffer?"

He paused, apparently thinking out his answer, unfazed and unwavering in his regard of her.

"Several very good, and very important reasons, none of which you need to be worried about as none are any sort of threat to you." That quirky little half-smile flashed, this time with a hint of apology. "I know you don't know me, but you know Castor, and he knows me very well. Trust him."

There were some undertones and subtleties in that first sentence that definitely needed clarification. What was so important to both men that they did something this extreme? She waited, leaving an expectant silence, but he didn't seem inclined to fill it. Well, as soon as he left she'd do some research.

She moved on to the second question. "Are you gay? Because, honestly, I'd prefer it if you were."

To her surprise, he didn't take offense, confirm, or laugh it off. Instead, the grey of his eyes darkened to storms and his mouth twisted into something almost scornful but not quite - as if he were disappointed by the question, by her.

He tugged her closer and let go of her hand to slide his slowly down her back until her hips pressed against his thigh and she had to lift her face to see his. With his other hand he traced one finger along the line of her fringe, down one cheek, lightly down the length of her neck and across a collarbone, stopping just short of her breast.

Kali couldn't help the sudden thudding of her heart, the catch of her breath as her lungs stopped working, the flush of warmth as her body reacted of its own accord to his closeness. She breathed in his warm scent and her knees weakened. It took every ounce of self-discipline not to reach up and pull his head down; not to kiss him senseless. Why she resisted she wasn't sure, except that his near-arrogant response to her question annoyed her as much as it aroused her.

His mouth hovered mere inches from hers, his breath sweet with butter chicken and beer, gaze sparking as it rested briefly on her mouth.

"What do you think, Kali?"

She stayed perfectly still. Her left hand came to rest on his bicep. She fought the overpowering urge to slide it over his bronzed skin, underneath the shirt. The hard bulge pushing against her hip bone left her in no doubt of his physical interest. Not gay, then. The question was: what did she do now?

He'd played the sex card way too soon and with a confidence just skirting the edge of disinterested arrogance - as though he knew he was attractive, was used to women throwing themselves at him and was not above picking and choosing and tossing aside. She did not want to be just one more, no matter how much her body raged at her to throw caution to the wind.

"I think," she said, slanting a calculating look under her lashes, "that you're far too sure of yourself, Mr Schiffer. I think," she added as his expression closed up into cold distance, "that you need to let me go before you lose something you probably value. Because, in case you didn't know, Kali *is* the Hindu goddess of death and destruction. Just a warning."

His body tensed for a second then he let her go and moved back a half-step, glancing down. Waiting long enough to be sure he'd seen it, Kali calmly tucked the lethal little knife she'd held at groin height back into its hidden sheath in her boot and twitched her pants cuff into place. The flush in her cheeks probably gave away her discomfort but she returned his cool look with an equally icy one of her own.

"Interesting," he said. "I do believe having you on this trip will be more valuable than I anticipated. See you in the morning, then." With a mock salute, he spun on his heel and exited, running lightly down the stairs. At the bottom, he looked back. "By the way, if you're going to act a part, you need to maintain the accent."

Without waiting for a reply, he roared off in a black Porsche nine-eleven - what a surprise.

Kali closed the door, considering it for awhile before heading into her home-office. Dropping into an office chair, she spun slowly in a circle. What was her next move? There was something...odd going on. Something clearly involving Castor as more than just as an Ebay seller. She had no proof, just a gut feeling; a connection she'd always shared with her brother. Something twanged that feeling now and she needed to pay attention to it. Her instincts about people were generally spot on and her instincts about Alex Schiffer said he was trouble - just what kind she wasn't quite sure yet. It could just be her own self-protectiveness kicking in - trying to prevent her from getting involved with someone so clearly used to control and power.

On the other hand, it could be something entirely different. He'd said having her on the trip would be more *valuable*. Not more fun, more enjoyable, more entertaining or any other lighthearted word. More *valuable*. As though she were an asset of some sort; of some use rather than just a joyride or a girl for hire. What was that about? Did he have something over Castor? Had he forced Castor to let him win the auction? But to what end?

She needed more information. She tossed the cowboy hat aside and pulled her phone out. Thumbing to Castor's number she hit Dial and waited. Voicemail. He was either dodging her or in a meeting - either was possible.

Switching on her laptop, she accessed a secure site courtesy of a friend in the police force and punched in Alex Schiffer's licence number - one of the benefits to having a near-photographic memory. After a few seconds searching, a single page of information came up. Clean. Totally clean. A man who owned a Porsche but had no speeding fines or red light fines? Not even a parking ticket. Really? Was he some sort of saint? His warm hands and sultry amusement flashed to mind. No, definitely not a saint. What, then?

She did some more digging. The web was full of useless information on Alex Schiffer. Gossip and innuendo, not much of substance. Age thirty-one. Australian born to a German father and Egyptian mother - that accounted for the tan, then. University educated with a degree in Chemical Engineering. Made his money in his early twenties with several patents in environmental chemistry improvements adopted by governments all over the world. Currently working as a consultant engineer on exclusive projects, all with an environmental slant. Man with green tendencies? Or just someone who knew where the next trend was coming from?

Apparently single but with a string of women photographed hanging off his arm and exposing their cleavages to the cameras. She stifled an unexpected surge of disappointment. She'd already suspected he was a player, hadn't she? Why did it surprise her? She reviewed the images again, trying to see them dispassionately. Oddly enough, most of the photos showed the girlfriends clearly but Alex only in partials - always covered by a hand, a piece of paper, a hat, facing the wrong way. Just bad luck?

Was she just being overly suspicious? Surely it was odd, even for someone as obviously wealthy as Alex Schiffer, to spend almost four hundred thousand on the privilege of flying one more girl to an island. A girl he'd never even met. OK, so if you left out the sexy photo on Ebay; if you left out the girl altogether, what did that leave for him to be interested in? The island? Someone on the island? Who? Amy? Was he a celebrity-stalker?

As Castor had rightly pointed out, Amy was famous and her fiancé wealthy. Was Alex with the media? Was he just using Castor and herself to get to the island to cover an otherwise off-limits wedding? A fillip of disappointment fluttered through her belly at the thought. She shoved it aside. If she left out her own ego, it was really the only thing that made sense. Or did it?

She skimmed again through the websites. No mention anywhere of any connection with media. In fact, she paused at one story, there was a mention of Alex taking one journalist to court for invasion of privacy. So maybe not then. What? What was his reason for doing this? It just didn't make any sense.

Kali tried Castor again but with no luck. She placed three other calls to various useful people but got no joy there, either. Alex Schiffer led an apparently blameless life; not a scandal or secret to be found. Not even an angry ex-girlfriend revealing his dirty sex secrets. Throwing the phone aside, she growled at it and shut the laptop with a snap. This was getting nowhere. Everyone had secrets. Alex was clearly better than most at hiding them.

Yanking the hairties out of her braids, she tried to drag ideas from her head by running her fingers through the wavy locks. No good. Every way she came at it, she just didn't have enough information to understand what was going on.

To relieve her frustration, she fired off a quick querying email to her brother, requesting more information on Alex. He'd called him a friend but she had no recollection of his name ever being mentioned. That didn't necessarily mean anything, as she and Castor lead busy lives and only saw each other maybe once or twice a month for a catch up or dinner with their parents. Castor may have dismissed his career 'in marketing' quite casually but he was one of the movers and shakers in the multinational corporation he worked for.

She sat back and stretched. There wasn't much more she could do, except pack. She'd lied to Castor about having an appointment, so her time was free. She deliberately put Schiffer out of mind and wandered back out into the kitchen, startled to find the afternoon well-advanced; the golden, dusty light streaming through the back windows to illuminate the jewel-like colours of a stained glass creation she had hung there only weeks before. She paused to admire it, screwing up her nose at the scruffy, untidy back yard beyond. She really needed to hire a gardener when she got back.

Nine whole days! Leaning her hands on the kitchen bench, she examined the wedding invitation pinned to the fridge. Who on earth had a wedding celebration lasting over a week? She'd tried to convince Amy to shorten it and to need her chief bridesmaid for just two days, but to no avail. She was requested to be on the island tomorrow for first rehearsal and then the hens' night was due to start at lunch on Monday and who knew when that would end. In between that and the actual wedding on Thursday morning, Amy planned a series of events, functions and entertainments to keep everyone busy. There was even a full masquerade ball on Tuesday night, with costume provided, for God's sake. It was over the top.

Running a finger down the list, Kali did a quick mental inventory. She did not have enough shoes and clothes to compete with the A-list women who would be there. Not even if she took her whole closet. Nor did she have time, funds or inclination to go shopping. Was it too late to cancel altogether? Yes, it was. Amy would be completely and justifiably devastated if she got that phone call and it wasn't some sort of dire emergency. They'd been best friends since they were twelve. Neither distance nor different career paths in separate countries had broken their bond, no matter how thin circumstances had stretched it. Kali couldn't let her down.

So it appeared her only option was to go with Alex tomorrow. At least she'd find out what he was up to.

Snatching the invitation off the fridge, she strode back into her bedroom and yanked a large suitcase out of the bottom corner of her wardrobe. Shoving back in the welter of shoes, belts and random forgotten stuff avalanching out along with it, she threw the case onto the bed and flipped the lid open.

Next she pushed all the hanging clothing to one end and, with event list in hand, began to inspect each item, scraping the metal hangers along the pole with increasing frustration. This was ridiculous - black tie dinners every night, the rehearsal, the hens night, breakfasts and lunches. She pulled out a few items: two pairs of bikinis and a one-piece - none of them glamorous but all nice enough. Three sarongs went in next, along with a couple of floppy hats, sunglasses, underclothing, casual clothing and various other paraphernalia.

When she couldn't put off the selection any longer, she moved on to more formal wear. Holding herself sternly together, she carefully folded half a dozen shining, bejewelled gowns and cursed her stupidity. She'd sworn she wouldn't wear them again but had never been able to bring herself to get rid of them. Now that decision returned to haunt her.

By the time she'd added shoes, purses, makeup and jewelry to the collection, the suitcase bulged. Hopefully the resort would be able to press any creases out. She didn't want to take more than one case of clothes. Her camera case was large enough on its own to be a second suitcase.

At last she was done, decisions made, case zipped and waiting. She hefted it to the floor, doubting again the wisdom of going.

Her phone rang. She read the screen and smiled. Amy.

"Hallo bride-to-be, how's things in paradise?" She sat on the bed, leaned back and put her feet up on the suitcase.

"I can't *wait* for you to get here, Kali," Amy gushed. "You won't *believe* this place."

Kali laughed. "All dayspas and swim up bars, I suppose? Just your thing, I know."

"All that and more." Amy's perpetual good humour transcended any electronic device. "You'll love it here too. I know you don't go for the girlie stuff but I promise there's enough to keep you interested for at least a week."

"Does it have to be a whole week, Ames?" She was glad to have a chance to put the question to her again. "I do have a business to run, y'know. I can't afford to be away a whole week."

"Yes, it does," Amy replied tartly. "I know you: you work yourself half to death, never have any fun and live like a nun. I even considered paying you to be my photographer because I knew you'd complain like this. But if I do that you won't relax at all. You need to get your ass over here and party. Besides, this is the perfect place to pick up clients for your business - lots of rich people coming, I promise. Some very hot single young guys, too."

"Quit it, Amy," Kali sighed. "The very last thing I need is a rich young guy. I'm twenty-seven. Besides, Caz already set me up with one. You'll never believe this."

She went on to tell Amy about Castor's Ebay ploy and, predictably, Amy thought the whole thing a huge joke and a brilliant idea.

Something in her tone was off, though.

"You already knew about it, didn't you?" Kali said, sitting up on the bed.

Amy's throaty laugh confirmed her suspicion. "Of course. With only a couple days left to the festivities, do you think I'd let my chief bridesmaid get stuck in Brisbane? It was my idea, silly. Max's jet is tied up hopping back from Malaysia, bringing his whole family and his best man, so I had to come up with something! You've been celibate and single for too long. It's time to move on."

"I think I may have to kill you," Kali stated.

Amy laughed again. "You'll have to come here to do it then, sweetie. I'll be waiting. Can't wait to meet your date. He sounds hot. See you tomorrow." She signed off with another chuckle, before Kali could retort.

She swore at the phone and tossed it aside. Next steps: dinner, finish packing, sleep. In that order. It was going to be a long week.

Chapter Three

Slightly over eighteen hours later, Kali strapped herself firmly into the copilot seat of a distinctly upmarket jet and watched with grudging admiration as Alex Schiffer prepared efficiently for takeoff. She remained silent as he communicated with the tower, taxied down the runway and launched them smoothly into the air. Once he'd levelled off and set the autopilot, she finally spoke, her voice breathy in the headset.

"So, when Caz said you had a Lear jet, I sort of assumed it would be a hire with a pilot up here and us in the back sipping champagne." She raised an eyebrow at him in mock superciliousness.

Alex didn't rise to the bait, but replied simply, "I'm sure you don't want to be stuck on an island for a week if the party is a complete washout. Besides, I like to have control over my exits."

"Ahh, control-freak?" She pursed her mouth and folded her arms.

He pushed a couple more buttons. "Only over myself. I'm under no illusions about my ability to control anyone else. Manipulate, possibly; control, no, but manipulating people has such ugly connotations and consequences, don't you think?"

Kali stiffened and blinked in surprise. A man with self-awareness? Unlikely. Was he implying he was manipulating her or she him? Probably both. Or, more likely, neither. She had a tendency to overthink things.

She checked out the window but there were only fluffy white clouds below. Nothing to pretend to watch. Instead, hands folded in her lap, she inspected the insane array of dials and blinking lights in front of them. She'd always wanted to learn to fly but never had the funds or time. It was a rich man's game.

"Did you get time for breakfast?" His polite question interrupted her scornful thoughts.

She shook her head, studying his profile critically.

Why did her ideas about him trend toward the skeptical and cynical? Probably because he just seemed too good to be true: gorgeous, rich, intelligent, sexy, straight. There must be a catch. There always was. Nobody so perfect stayed single. He must have some fatal flaw. The trick was, finding it before she made any dumb mistakes - like sleeping with him.

She was not stupid, nor inexperienced. The tzing of serious chemistry between them was impossible to miss, as were the signs of his interest. She'd operated on heightened awareness of his every move since she first stepped onto the plane. Every motion he made, every slight change of expression, every flicker of humour; she reacted, physically. Even more annoyingly, she caught herself dwelling on x-rated fantasies; wondering how he would be in bed.

She dug her nails into her palms, trying to get a grip. It was just millions of years of mating instinct trying to tell her to have sex with and impress a compatible male. Nothing more. She'd been burned by that instinct before and was disinclined to let it govern her choices again. Hard to keep that in the forefront of her mind, though, when he sat only inches away and every shift of muscle under that black tshirt made her want to rip it off him.

"Well," he continued, apparently responding to her

reply about breakfast, "it's a good thing I had them stock the plane last night. Let's go see what we have." He hung his headset up, unbuckled and left the cockpit. Kali followed.

What the hell had she got herself into?

There wasn't room in the tiny galley for two people, so she sat at a nearby dining table, as Alex prepared, with quiet competence, an omelette. He seemed absorbed in the task, barely acknowledging her after he'd asked her preferences. He was fascinating to watch. He had a smooth, lithe economy of movement; a languid air of confidence. He showed none of the normal male attributes of needing to boast about himself and his toys for her to ooh and aah over. In fact he didn't seem to want to impress her at all, which was most unusual - and most refreshing.

Although she'd told Castor she didn't care about her appearance, that wasn't true. In her late teens and early twenties she went through the phase of dressing to kill and being pursued by men because of it. Doing so led to the most painful episode of her life. One she still tried hard to forget. As a result, she'd downplayed her looks for the last few years, partly in an effort to be taken seriously in her commercial photographic work, partly to deflect male attention until she was good and ready. It didn't always work, so it was quite nice, in some ways, to be with someone who didn't seem to want her to fawn over him in admiration; or to dribble over her like a lovestarved teenager.

Alex made it clear, yesterday, he found her attractive but he seemed content to leave it at that. In the light of the photos of him with women hanging off his arms, perhaps the net gossip was wrong. Perhaps he wasn't single after all?

A plate came to rest on the table in front of her, startling her out of her musings. Alex slid into the seat opposite and laid a fork and knife down for her.

"Salt's in the little cupboard by your left elbow, if you want it." He applied himself to his own food without awaiting her 'thankyou'.

He ate with the same focus that he seemed to bring to everything. Self-contained; quietly-confident; independent best described him so far. It remained to be seen if that was just a front or went deeper. In her experience, most confident men needed the people around them to act as a sort of admiring audience, reflecting back their own magnificence to them. The jury was still out on Alex.

After breakfast, they sat on plush couches, in the middle of the plane, sipping coffee and saying little. The hum of the engines filled the silence. Occasionally Alex checked a digital display showing, presumably, their flight status and details. It was reassuring that he kept watch. Flying on autopilot thousands of metres above the ocean was a little disconcerting.

He put his cup in a holder by the couch and stretched his legs out. Today he wore a fitted black tshirt that moulded to his upper body, and grey cargo shorts revealing beautifully sculpted calves. Kali glanced away, annoyed with herself for noticing. It was just hard not to.

"You don't talk much, do you?" Alex's amused, deep voice intruded on her thoughts.

She fiddled with the handle on her cup. "Neither do you."

He chuckled. "True, but it's supposed to be a female trait, isn't it? The need to fill silences with words? According to personal development writers like Alan Pease, women have about twenty thousand words a day to get out, on average."

She put her cup down and stretched out to mirror his pose on the opposite couch. "Maybe I'm not average, and maybe that's pretty damned sexist."

"Touché." He inclined his head in acknowledgement. "Although I'm not sure pointing out measurable differences between male and female counts as sexist. I just hope your reticence isn't because you're afraid of me or anything? After all, we did have a rather...unusual introduction."

She sent him an ironic look. "You could call it that but no, I'm not afraid of you. Why *did* you bid for this trip?"

He sucked a quick breath and leaned forward, intense with sudden curiosity, elbows resting on his knees as he studied her. He ignored her question. "No, you're not afraid are you? Not even slightly intimidated. Why is that?"

She couldn't help but laugh. "What is it with rich men? Why do you all think women should dissolve into a blithering heap of brainless hero worship when you walk into a room?"

Alex's mouth twisted into a dry smile as he leaned back again. "Probably because most do. So why are you different?"

Kali rolled her eyes and threw in some sarcasm for good measure. "Oh, I'm not really. I'm just playing hard to get so you'll find me intriguing. Honestly, what an arrogant, narcissistic, and *definitely* sexist statement, followed by a dumb question. If you really think that, you're hanging around the wrong women. Not all women are waiting to be rescued by some mythical knight in shining armour and I've learned from past mistakes." The instant she said it, she regretted the words. It would only lead to questions she wasn't prepared to answer.

Surprisingly, the next words out of his mouth were not the predictable ones. Instead, he tilted his head to one side and, with the merest hint of a twinkle of humour, he asked,

"Are you gay? Honestly, I'd prefer it if you weren't."

She froze for a second in shock. Oh, wait, her question to him the day before. He was just playing games. Two could do that, although it wasn't her normal modus operandi. She stayed away from men who played mindgames. For some reason though, Alex Schiffer annoyed the heck out of her. She also got the impression he did it deliberately. Well, two could do that. Let's see if she could rattle his seemingly unflappable calm; push back and offbalance him enough to get a genuine reaction; something to reveal who hid underneath that cool exterior. And what he really wanted.

Reaching a, possibly-stupid, decision, she eased off the couch, bridged the gap in two swaying steps and straddled his lap, her knees on either side of his thighs, her backside resting on his thighs. His expression was even more amused now. He didn't move as, with one finger, she traced a line across his forehead, along one cheek, down his neck and across his collarbone. She flattened her palm against the broad strength of his pectoral muscle. It jumped beneath her hand. Leaning down, she held her mouth an inch away from his and whispered,

"What do you think, Alex? Am I gay? Kiss me and find out."

For a moment, electricity and tension sparked between them. Without moving, all humour gone, he returned her look with such assessing, beguiling intensity that Kali was held captive. Here was no simple, sex-driven rich guy after a quick lay. This was a complex, intelligent man with a history possibly as painful as her own. He was just better at playing the game than she; better at detaching his deeper emotions from his relationships; better at keeping his distance mentally, if not physically.

Shaken, she leaned back. This was not a man she wanted to get involved with. He would either use her in the same way he had all those women she'd seen him with on Google, or things would get way too serious and she would get hurt - again. There was no way she could risk that.

She transferred her weight, sliding one leg off the couch. Alex, who had not moved since she sat down, smiled; this time with a hint of sadness that surprised her even more. He let her go without touching her and she sat beside him on the couch, unable to fathom what had just happened. Why hadn't he kissed her? Most men would have. She'd felt his arousal between her thighs; seen the dilation of his pupils, the quickening breath. Yet he did nothing. What the hell? She was both relieved and, perversely, annoyed.

He hitched one leg up onto the couch, shifting to face her. He reached out a hand and trailed the back of his fingers down her cheek, his expression one of faint interest with, again, that hint of melancholy. The touch sent a shiver of pleasure across her skin.

"I think," he leaned closer, cupping the back of her head, his fingers twining sensuously through her loose hair, "that you are," he pulled her toward him, his lips only inches away from hers now, "a fascinating woman, who has been badly hurt and is yet to tap into her own power." Swiftly, as though aware she was about to pull away, he kissed her.

It lasted only a moment, just a warm, fleeting brush of his lips on hers, but it sent a sharp spike of tingling desire, a rush of hot excitement, through her body that made Kali jerk away in sudden fear. Before she could even voice a protest or fight against him, he was gone - his touch, his lips, his whole person. He rose smoothly from the couch and vanished into the cockpit without another word, leaving her gasping for breath, heart hammering, stunned by the intensity of her body's reaction to his touch.

She stayed where she was for a few minutes, until the adrenalin rush died and her hands stopped shaking. What the hell was that about? Yet to tap into her own power? What a stupid, head-game sort of thing to say. Angry at herself and at him for playing with her emotions that way, she shoved off the couch then paused, studying the back of his head through the cockpit door.

That sense of unease from yesterday stole over her again. He *was* toying with her emotions but to what end?

He'd dodged her question about the ebay auction. He'd also never been in any danger of losing control. Yes, clearly he was turned on by her but everything about him screamed tight emotional control and ruthless focus. He had an agenda alright and part of it involved keeping *her* offbalance so she wouldn't ask awkward questions.

Right, so she'd have to just be a little smarter about it.

Slipping into the copilot seat again, she put on the headset. Far below, the clouds vanished and only the featureless, blue-grey, white-flecked ocean surface extended in all directions.

"How much longer?"

"About fifteen minutes," he responded calmly. "We're about to start our descent. Want to take the stick?"

"What? No!" Her reply was automatic, fear-based.

She snapped her mouth shut, dismayed at her reaction. She tried not to voice her first thoughts, as they were often wrong. She was a glass half-empty kind of person but that didn't mean she had to like it or allow it to dominate her thinking. So she took a deep breath and blew it out to calm her racing heart.

"Actually, I take that back. I've always wanted to learn. What do I do?"

With a flicker of a smile, Alex talked her through the basics. Watching the horizon indicator, she began the descent, her heart hammering so loud in her ears she thought her eardrums would burst. With Alex's calm instructions and encouragement, she brought them down to within visual range of the island. Next he had her bank to the right and begin a long, spiralling approach to the short landing strip.

"Is this how you normally come in to land?" she asked, incredulous as they circled a third time, lower over the island. It seemed like a slow way to get to the ground. She couldn't see much because the island lay below his side. He kept his attention on the ground now easily visible to him.

"No, but I thought you might enjoy a few more minutes of flying time. Now, when you come around again we'll be about ready to line up for landing and I'll take over."

Sweat beaded on her forehead and trickled down her spine. Straightening the wheel she released it with relief on his say-so. Flexing cramped fingers, she admired his skill as he lined up the landing strip with precision and brought the jet down with hardly a bump. They taxied toward the tiny terminal and drew to a halt in front of a decent sized hangar.

Alex inclined his head a fraction. "Nice job for your first flight."

Kali huffed a huge breath and laughed as the rush and excitement of what she'd done hit. Her hands trembled as she took off the headset. He removed his as well. Pressing cold fingers to her flushed cheeks, she grinned at him.

"That was *fun*. Thankyou!"

He paused in the middle of flicking off a switch, an arrested expression on his face. His hand closed into a fist, then he swung away but not before she saw his jaw clench.

"You're welcome." His tone was calm but with an inexplicable edge of something like anger to it. "The tower said they're sending a car for us and will take our bags as well, so you go on ahead and I'll finish up here. The handle on the door will open it." He didn't look her way again; didn't acknowledge as she slid out of the cockpit and grabbed her handbag. He focussed on something on the instrument panel, flicking switches and making notes in a logbook.

Unable to fathom what bothered him, Kali opened the door and waited as it extended steps with a hiss of compressed air and a whirr of electronics. A light breeze blew up, dispersing the scent of avgas. She drew a deep breath, savouring the smell of frangipani, saltwater and greenery.   Warm tropical sunshine bathed her uplifted face as she squinted into the blue sky and adjusted her sunglasses on her nose. The crunch of tyres on gravel drew her attention downward to where a golf cart bounced across the tarmac toward the jet. It whined to a halt at the base of the steps and a young, smartly-dressed man of maybe eighteen or twenty got out and smiled up at her.

"Welcome. If you'd like to come down, ma'am, I'll take you straight to your room so you can freshen up and relax before tonight's rehearsal dinner."

She stepped down as he opened the cargo hold and pulled out her bags and two large, silvery suitcases she assumed belonged to Alex. The boy placed them on the luggage rack of the cart and waved her into the passenger seat. As she climbed in, Alex ran down the stairs then pressed a button on a remote of some sort and watched as they folded back up. He swung himself into the rear passenger seat with a nod for their driver.

"I'm Jason, ma'am, sir. I'll be your butler for the duration of your stay. If you need anything at all, you just call me." The boy grinned at Kali as he accelerated away from the plane.

"OK," she replied faintly, a little overwhelmed at the thought of having a butler. "Anything?"

"Anything ma'am," he affirmed. "Any time of day or night. The resort prides itself on its ability to have or get whatever you need as fast as possible. We have our own cargo plane."

"OK," she repeated, stunned. "So what's the weirdest request you've ever had then?"

Jason smiled ruefully, all white teeth, tan and blond good looks. "Sorry ma'am, we all sign a confidentiality agreement, so I can't tell you. I'm sure you understand."

"Oh, of course." Dumb question. This was an insanely exclusive private island. Of course he had to sign a confidentiality paper. "Can you at least stop calling me ma'am? I'm Kalisa, Kali for short. If you're going to be waiting on me, I'd rather you called me by name."

"Sorry ma'am." He gave her an apologetic shrug. "House rules. More than my job's worth. Is Miss Brooker suitable?"

"No," she growled, "it makes me sound like a schoolteacher. Oh, for…" She twisted in her seat to look back at Alex, "is this how you travel?"

From behind dark glasses, he smiled faintly. "Isn't it interesting to see how the other half live?"

She screwed up her nose at him. What did she make of that comment? He was good at dodging direct answers to direct questions.

Chapter Four

The drive to the resort took longer than she expected and showed the island to be more extensive than she'd thought. As they wound through forested hills, she caught glimpses of a golf course, something that might be a go-kart track, an archery range and, in the distance, the distinctive popping of gunfire echoed. A shooting range perhaps? A pair of hang gliders circled over the beach, their red and white geometric wings brilliant against the blue sky. Jetskis and speedboats left white trails looping across the glittering ocean.

Then, when the cart zipped over the crest of a small range of hills that ran down the spine of the island, a perfect little cove came into view and she gasped in delighted surprise. Before her spread the idyllic paradise of every postcard; the white-sand, coconut palm, blue-water brilliance every tropical resort promised and few delivered.

Nestled discreetly amongst the trees were little thatch-roofed cottages, each with balconies, broad windows and, apparently, all the mod-cons delivered by electricity. Service buildings, assuming they existed, were so well hidden that Kali couldn't spot them at all. They did pass a squash court, tennis courts and a building labelled 'spa'. Amy would be in heaven. She wouldn't even notice the rest of the facilities existed. Clearly 'island retreat' didn't mean roughing it in the rich-people world.

Jason pulled the cart up in front of a cottage tucked away at the end of a fragrant, tree-lined boulevard and handed over a key and two keycards.

"This one is for the cart and these are for the cottage doors. If you'll follow me, I'll show you the facilities."

From the back seat, Alex reached through and took the keys. "That's fine, thanks Jason. We'll work it out."

"I'll get your bags then, sir." The boy jumped out of the cart and collected the bags. He led the way into the house, shouldering the door open and depositing the suitcases carefully in a ridiculously large walk in wardrobe in the hall. Alex escorted him to the door with a murmur of thanks and closed it behind him.

Kali wandered through the villa. It, too, was larger than she'd expected. Once through the short entry hall, it opened into a vast open-plan living and kitchen area with a magnificent view of the beach and vibrant turquoise water only a few metres away. The furnishings were a luxurious 'beach-house' style - muted blues and creams with splashes of tropical colour in the silk cushions, artwork and rugs. One wall sported a huge fishtank in place of where a television would normally be.

Tropical fish flashed brilliant colour as they flickered back and forth in the tank. Next to it stood a bookshelf, prestocked with at least a hundred novels of all sorts and genres. No television anywhere visible. Nice. A week without the news would actually be kind of a relief. Outside the glass sliding doors, a wide verandah held outdoor furniture and a sheltered, covered four-person spa, hidden in a cosy nook designed for romantic liaisons at midnight. She spun away, opening a door to what turned out to be a bedroom. It housed a massive, king-sized bed, an ensuite, dressing table, sitting area and another huge closet. Clearly this place catered to people who travelled with extensive wardrobes.

She re-entered the living area to find Alex sitting on a

breakfast barstool, leaning back with his elbows on the counter, watching her. That slight, intriguing aura of calm humour was back. He seemed to have regained total control. She suppressed a silly urge to poke her tongue at him. Instead she scanned the four walls of the living area again. There were no more doors.

"One bedroom."

"So it would appear," he returned, with a hint of teasing laughter.

"That's fine." She shrugged. "It looks like the couches convert to beds. I'll sleep there."

"Suit yourself." He eased himself off the stool and disappeared into the hall, reappearing with all three suitcases and her camera bag. Taking them into the bedroom he deposited hers and one of his in the wardrobe. The other he dropped onto the bed and flipped open. Apparently ignoring her, he proceeded to hold a tuxedo up for critical inspection.

Kali ground her teeth. Of course he didn't do the chivalrous thing and give the bed up to her. Why did she expect him to be predictable? Hadn't she already decided he intended to keep her off balance?

She stalked into the bathroom and rummaged in the cupboards. Not finding what she wanted, she went to the hall and checked there. Still nothing.

'What are you hunting for?" Alex's voice drifted out of the bedroom

"Iron and ironing board," she said.

There was a laugh from the other room. He emerged to lean casually against the door frame. "Can you picture the people who come here actually ironing their own clothing? Or even owning clothes that can be ironed?"

She snorted. "Of course. Silly me." Snatching up the house phone, she dialled Jason's extension. He answered first ring.

"Hi. Sorry to bug you but would you please arrange to

have someone press my evening dresses, Jason? I'll need at least one ready for this evening - around three o'clock if that's ok? Great, thanks."

She placed the phone on its cradle and retrieved her case from the wardrobe. Placing it on the opposite side of the bed, she ignored Alex as she unpacked, placing her own things methodically away in the various drawers and hangers available. Her scant attire took up barely any space in the enormous wardrobe, but too bad. She'd make do. He unpacked only one case. The other he tucked away in the back of the closet. It had padlocks on it.

A minute later, Jason arrived and carefully accepted her dresses and Alex's suits with a cheerful salute and a promise to return the selected garments before three. It was only eleven am. He offered suggestions for lunch as well, mentioning the room service or a beachside restaurant a short walk away. As an afterthought, as he left, he reminded her that everything was already paid for.

Shaking her head at the extravagance, Kali wandered around the villa, touching things without really seeing them, inspecting the brilliantly-coloured fish in the tank, restless and lost without a schedule and a pile of things to do. The beach called to her, begged her to bring her camera and capture its tropical perfection.

"Drink?" Alex stood by the fridge, holding up a soft drink.

She accepted it gratefully. She was thirsty and, since the mention of lunch, hungry.   In the warm air, water condensed on the bottle, chilling her fingers and dripping onto her green t-shirt.

The room phone rang, melodious and quietly intrusive. She jumped.   Alex answered, his tone laconic and responses brief.

"It was your friend, Amy." He put it down and took a swig of his drink. "She asked if you could stop by around two just to say Hi before the dinner. Apparently she's got a bunch of her fiance's relatives flying in now and has to entertain them for awhile. She apologised."

Kali folded her arms. "You should have handed it over. She's *my* friend."

"Yes, you're right. I apologise." He sank onto a couch, curiosity in his grey eyes now. "Tell me about Amy. How'd you two meet?"

"Um..." Thrown offguard by his ready apology, she took a moment to gather her thoughts, dropping into an amazingly comfortable couch opposite. She kicked off her runners, put white-sock-clad feet up across a corner of the glass and timber coffee table and slouched into the cushions.

"We met in Science in our first year of high school. I figured anyone who wore pink, heart-shaped reading glasses and blue-sequinned sunglasses had to be fun to hang out with. I was right. She's a blast. We've been friends ever since, even though we don't see much of each other now she's on the big screen." She leaned back, tossing down the last of her drink. "One of those friendships where you can pick up the phone and know you'll take up just where you left off. You know?"

"I know." A flicker of something suspiciously like pain showed, just for an instant; gone so fast that its existence wasn't certain. "And how did Amy meet her fiancé, Max Chan, isn't it?"

His expression was as calm as ever but his body held the merest hint of tension now. She set the bottle down on the coffee table with a click and leaned back again, folding her arms across her chest.

"Tell you what, how about we play tag? I answer a question if you answer one as well. Deal?"

Alex paused in mid-sip, lowered his drink to the table and leaned forward. "How about we go get some lunch? I'm starving."

Kali jumped to her feet, hands on hips. Showdown

time. "No. Enough is enough. I don't know you, Alex. You bought the right to deliver me to this island but there was nothing on that Ebay sale that said I had to let you stay. If you're not going to tell me what your agenda is, then you can get the hell out of here. I will *not* take a complete stranger into my best friend's wedding without knowing more about why you're here. I'm not an idiot. I can see you're hiding something. If you want to spend another minute here, you'd better cough up and it'd better be something I can verify."

He leaned back again, his expression thoughtful as he linked hands across his stomach. There was a long silence as he apparently considered his response. He waved a hand at the couch.

"OK, sit down and we'll do a deal, but first we need to call your brother."

Taken by surprise, she sat back down on the soft, cream leather with a thump. "Caz? Why on earth do we need to talk to him?"

He tilted his head, his eyes flashing secret amusement. "Clearance to tell you what I need to tell you."

"Clearance? What the...? Oh. My. God." She stared at him as the pieces fell into place. "Are you serious? *My* brother...my *brother* is with...who, ASIO?...and I didn't even know? That...bastard!" It all made sense now - the overseas trips, the rapid rise in the company he worked for, the trips to Sydney and Canberra. What a sneak!

"I can't believe he never told me - or that they took someone like him!" She growled. "He's so...so...impulsive and irresponsible!"

Alex grinned, his whole aspect lightening. "I am beginning to think you should've been recruited as well. Actually he's with ASIS - the overseas intelligence branch."

"And you?" Kali studied him. He was much more her idea of a spy than Castor. "Where do you fit in?"

"I'm...well, let's just say I'm a consultant with a special interest in this particular case." The lightness fell away in an instant.

"So you're not some sort of super-rich eccentric businessman who bought a lift to a wedding for the fun of it?" She eyed him narrowly, annoyed at the deception but glad, in many ways, that he might not be part of the high-flying world Google had portrayed for him.

"The fun of it? Hardly." His expression segued into irony and he jerked his chin at her. "Call Caz and ask him how much I can tell you."

She thumbed the speed dial on her phone and handed it over, still unable to comprehend how her flighty brother had kept such a huge secret from her. After Alex's short and rather cryptic conversation, she took the phone back.

"Is it true who you're working for?" She couldn't quite conceal the sibling petulance.

"Absolutely. Since Uni. It's a blast." His cheerful voice came down the line undaunted by her tone. "I've been meaning to talk to you about coming on board, actually. You'd be great with your skillset."

"Thanks ever so," she said sarcastically. "We'll talk when I get home, don't you worry."

"Ya, sure. Have fun. Hey," he sobered as she said goodbye, "Alex is a good guy. Like I said: I've known him for seven years. Stick with him and do what he says, ok? This is nothing dangerous but he knows he has to look after you."

"Why the hell couldn't you have told me this yesterday?"

His shrug was almost audible. "Would've been better if you never knew."

"Better for who?"

Caz laughed again but didn't answer, only bid her goodbye.

She thumbed the End button, swore at him and

growled in frustration at the phone in her hand before tossing it aside.

"So give. What's going on? Who are you?" She pointed an accusing finger at Alex. "Why are you here instead of Caz? He could easily have come as my plus one. Amy knows him."

"Yes," he agreed, "but he's in too important a position and is deeply involved in other things at the moment. He can't leave and we don't want to reveal who he is to Max if things go pear-shaped here."

"Max?" She jumped. "Max is who you're here for? What's he done? What are you trying to achieve? Is Amy in any danger?"

"One question at a time, shall we?" His tone was amused, that twisted little half-smile back.

"Any number of answers would be useful," she replied, folding her arms.

Alex drew a long, deep breath, stretched back, laced his hands behind his head and stared up at the ceiling. "Amy isn't in any danger right now but she may be getting herself into something she's not going to like."

She had to literally bite her tongue to stop herself from demanding more. Her natural impatience met its match in Alex. He was not the sort of man to be rushed by anyone. Besides, the sight of his muscular arms made her swallow, press her lips together and look away in an attempt not to get distracted.

He leaned forward again, regarding her intently. "Max Chang's real name is Chang Jiao-long. His family is Chinese Malay. He has a legitimate business front in construction but he makes more money moving drugs and selling people to the sex-slave-trade."

She gasped, her heart stuttering. She fisted a pillow in each hand, her head spinning with the possible implications. "And Amy? Does she know, do you think?"

He examined his own hands. "That's part of what I'm

here to find out - and I'm hoping you can help, since you know her. The challenge is: if she does know, is she involved?"

"Amy? Into drugs? No way!" Kali jumped to her friend's defence then shut her mouth. She hadn't seen Amy much since Max had come on the scene. They travelled a lot; Amy auditioned and worked in LA most of the previous year. In fact, this week would be the first time she'd seen Amy, in the flesh, for something like eight months. Anything could have happened in that time.

To his credit, Alex said nothing, merely watching her without expression or comment.

She let go her automatic denial and prompted him to continue. "What else are you here to find out then?"

"We believe Max is also using the drug and sex slave money to finance terrorist bases in Asia."

She let the first fear for Amy slide by so she could think clearly and shook her head.

"That one I'm certain Ames doesn't know about. Her brother was killed in action in Afghanistan, so I'm absolutely sure she wouldn't be part of that. So either it's not true, or she doesn't know. Either way," she cast Alex a level look, "I trust Castor and he trusts you, so you're right - we have to find out. What do you want me to do?"

"How well do you know Max?" He eyed her speculatively.

She tucked her feet up on the couch, hugging a pillow to her chest. "I've met him about a dozen times in the last two years they've been going out. Stayed at his place at the Gold Coast for a few days last year. He seemed ok." She screwed up her nose. "Although I have to admit that my first impression of him was that he was a bit sleazy. He made me uncomfortable for some reason. I guess I got used to him for Amy's sake. I haven't seen them for about eight months but I remember I used to be quite careful about not being alone with him."

He stayed silent, his lips pressed together, gazing at the fishtank over her shoulder, perfectly still but with white knuckles on his hands, clasped between his knees. What had she said to affect him so? She shivered at his blank, cold expression.

"Alex, what is it?"

He drew a slow breath, unclasped his hands and laid them on his knees instead, looking at her with calm inquiry. Something painful underlay the superficial tranquility he'd adopted.

Kali threw the cushion aside and moved across to sit next to him. "What is it about this whole thing that's so important to you?"

"What do you mean?" He met her gaze with cool indifference.

She studied him from under lowered lids. "You know what I mean. Based on your reactions and how you got here, I'd say you have not just a special interest, but a very *personal* interest in this."

He stilled but didn't speak, the tension in him marked by the utter motionlessness of his whole, lean body. She'd hit a nerve.

Her mind raced, forecasting a dozen different ways this scene could end if she played it wrong. She let a held breath out on a sigh and a shake of her head.

"I'd rather you trusted me to tell me, Alex. You owe me. I've trusted you so far on Caz's word but I won't help you if you've got some other agenda that's going to put either Amy, me, or you in any danger."

He raised his face to stare out the window but didn't reply. His knuckles whitened again.

"If I had to guess," she caught his gaze, putting pieces, hints and ideas together, "I'd say that this is incredibly, personally important - why else would anyone spend that much money just to get here? By your reactions to things I've said today, it's to do with someone close to you.

Maybe a very good friend." His hands twitched just a fraction, so she continued. "And maybe a woman; someone you loved; a sister or wife?"

With each word came just the very slightest reaction; just a tiny spasm of muscle around the jaw or eyes; so small most people wouldn't have seen it. She'd guessed near to the target.

She shifted closer and covered his hands with her own. "Tell me, Alex. What did Max do to her? To them?"

For just a second, his eyes blazed with such pain and anger that Kali jerked back, shocked. He shifted forward, following her motion, his nose just inches from hers. She leaned further until she lay against the cushions, feet still on the ground, her hands flat against his chest. He held himself above her, one hand on the couch-back, one on the cushions by her head. For the first time she almost feared of him, so intense was his expression.

"Caz was right about you," he murmured, eyes hard as they flicked to her mouth, "you're a regular Sherlock Holmes, aren't you?"

Chapter Five

The sexual tension, simmering in the background since they'd met, leapt to the fore again. Heat blossomed in Kali's face and belly. Her body flashed to life just through his proximity. She wanted nothing more than to slide her hands across the hard expanse of muscle under his t-shirt; to feel his skin shudder under her touch.

Slowly, Alex lowered his mouth to hers, watching her reaction.

This time it was no fleeting kiss; this time he was serious, skilled and sensual. She couldn't help the tiny whimper of desire that escaped her as his lips touched hers, warm and soft; teasing, gentle. She slid her hands around his body, arching her back to bring her breasts in contact with his broad chest. He deepened the kiss, taking her mouth with breathtaking passion and skill. Head swimming, heart pounding, body aching to be touched, she gave in to the desire to feel his skin and slipped her hands under his shirt. Warm, smooth, silken beneath her fingers, his sculpted muscles jumped at her touch. He groaned, low in his throat, nipping at her lower lip.

Their position was too awkward. She needed to see and feel more of him. She hooked her left arm around his elbow, lifted her hips and twisted, unbalancing him. He fell onto his back on the rug below the couch. Following, she landed astride his hips, palms flat on the woven rug beside him.   He stared up at her, alight with desire rather than pain.

He laid his hands on her hips, thumbs digging into the hollows.   Her body jerked in pleasurable reaction.   His hands slid under her shirt, dragging it off, over her head in one quick motion.   She tossed her wild hair back, enjoying the admiring glow in his eyes.   He splayed his fingers across her flat belly and she sucked a quick breath at the sensation of his calloused skin on hers.

"You are...unbelievably gorgeous," he murmured, caressing the heavy underside of her breasts.   His thumbs brushed across nipples hidden by white lace and Kali gasped, riding the rush of heat between her thighs.   She leaned forward, hair falling loose in a curtain about both their faces.

"And you," she kissed one corner of his mouth.   His hands slid around her back. "are very good...," she ran a trail of kisses down his jaw toward his ear.   He moved one bra strap off her shoulder.   "...at diversions and redirections."

His hand stilled, his harsh breathing ceased.

She stopped, sat up, tucked her hair behind her ears and hooked the bra strap up on her shoulder.   From his position on the ground, Alex looked back at her, impassive, unreadable once more.

"I'm not going to pretend I don't find you unbelievably sexy because I do," Kali admitted, tilting her head, "but I'm also not easily sidetracked.   When you've been manipulated by the best you learn to spot it a mile away."   She put her hands on her thighs.   "Why are you here, Alex?   What did Max do to you that makes you so determined to get to him?   You have to know that I *will* protect Amy and, at the moment, I don't know what your intention is or how it will hurt her."

He sighed, scrubbed one hand over his hair then his face, eyes closed.   She stayed where she was, unwilling to move in case she interrupted his train of thought. The coarse fibres of the rug dug into her knees. The hum of the airconditioner underpinned the moment with a heavy thrumming.

At last he opened his eyes. He was good at hiding but they echoed a memory of such torment that she had to resist the urge to throw her arms around him and tell him it would all be ok. He didn't need that from her - he needed help to slay whatever demons haunted him. Afterward, well...that was another matter. Right now, though, she wasn't prepared to either let him manipulate her with sex or to sleep with him just to satisfy her own raging libido.

"Ok." He sat up, wrapped one arm around her waist and hauled them both to their feet, depositing her on the couch as though she weighed no more than a suitcase. He swooped down and flicked her shirt across without comment. She slipped it over her head and tugged it to her waist, perching on the edge of the couch as he sat beside her.

"Can we at least order lunch?" He gave her a half-amused, half-plaintive look,

She folded her arms. "Fine, but no more put-offs or you can pack your bag and fly out today, agreed?"

"Agreed." He picked up the room service menu.

After a quick consultation, they agreed on a shared seafood platter and Alex called it in.

"Twenty minutes." He replaced the handset, his expression serious again.

"OK, give." Kali clenched her teeth, determined to have it out of him. "What's your involvement in this? Why is it so important?"

He stood, shoved his hands into his pants pockets and paced a few steps away. He stopped at the window, glancing out at the incongruously-beautiful view, though he probably saw none of it.

"I don't know all the details, you understand, so don't

ask me." He squared his shoulders and drew a deep breath. His eyes flat, he gazed at her, through her in fact. She shuddered at the sudden hardness in him.

"Five years ago my younger sister, Michelle, married my best friend, Jack Paulere. I was there for the wedding. Caz was there as well. That's why I went to him for help. I left to the USA on business a day or so later. Shelley and Jack went to Thailand and Malaysia for their honeymoon. The next I heard, they'd been kidnapped while on a walking tour in the highlands. I think they either strayed onto poppy-growing land or were followed and targeted. Either way, we got a ransom demand." He paused, his jaw working as he composed himself. Kali stayed silent, holding in her horror with difficulty. The story wasn't over.

"I would've paid to get them back," he continued, his voice bleak, "but I was too late. They didn't wait. Knowing Jack, I'd guess he tried to escape. He was ex-SAS. Their bodies were found just a few days later. Shelley had been...abused."

"Oh God," she breathed. "And how does Max fit into this?"

Alex raised his head, eyes stone and jaw iron. "It took me four years and a lot of money to gather enough information to connect Chang Jiao-Long to the murders and even then it's not anything I could prove in court. He's too powerful and people are too scared of him. The only way I can bring him to justice is to prove the terrorist, sex trade, or drug connections now. Preferably all three as I'd like him to go away forever. His security is so tight he's almost impossible to get near. We've tried three times to infiltrate his organisation but failed each time. Caz's people won't back me again if this falls through. It's costing them too many people and resources. This is my only shot."

"But," Kali opened her eyes wide at him, "won't he connect your name to Michelle's? Won't he know who you are as soon as he sees it?"

Alex shook his head and moved back to sit next to her on the couch. "Schiffer isn't my real name. Right now, I'm more concerned with how we're going to get information from Chang or Amy."

"So the history I Googled? Your licence? All Caz, right?" She pursed her lips. Castor owed her big time. She tried to lighten the mood a little. "I knew you were too clean to be real. And all those ridiculously busty models hanging off your arm? Really? Who are you?"

He ghosted a smile. "It doesn't matter. But," he reached out and cupped her chin with one lean hand, "I promise, when this is over, I'll tell you anything else you want to know about me." He brushed his thumb across her lips, his eyes softening briefly as they rested on her mouth.

"Stop it!" She shoved his hand away. "Stop trying to distract me with sex. If what you say is true then I'll help you. You don't have to try and influence me that way just to get what you want. Don't touch me again, alright? We're here on business now, nothing else." She shot to her feet and strode away to take his place at the verandah windows, both hurt and angry that he felt he still needed to control her in such an underhanded way - or at all.

Afternoon breezes whipped the sea into small, tumbling waves. Turquoise blue gave way to the dust-green of stirred up sand in the water. Purpling clouds gathered on the horizon, threatening rain, mimicking her mood.

A knock fell on the door and Jason entered, carrying a large tray. He placed it on the dining table and left again with a cheerful farewell. The sound of cutlery and the delicious wafting scent of seafood drew Kali to the table. She sat in silence, eating methodically, not enjoying the fabulous food as much as she might normally. All she could think of was Alex's sister and friend; of Amy; of how much of Alex was real and how much a mask he'd put on in the last five years to hide the pain; how much his closeness disturbed her; of what the hell the next five days would be like, constantly in his presence.

When she'd finished eating, she wiped her hands on the fine linen napkin and folded it in her lap. She cleared her throat, attempting to make her voice come out sounding normal, not squeaky and frightened – or even worse: husky and sexy.

"So, what's the plan? What are we trying to get out of Max and how do we get it?" She put an elbow on the table, chin on palm and waited expectantly.

He wiped his fingers and mouth and laid the napkin down on the table, leaning back and folding his hands across his stomach.

"Max came here on his yacht. Amy flew here to meet him two days ago. His family, I understand, are flying in any minute on his jet from Malaysia."

"So?" Kali lifted a shoulder. "How does that help?"

"I'd guess he and Amy are honeymooning either here or on the yacht. Do you know which?"

"Sure. She said they were having a few days here after the guests have gone, then the yacht back to Malaysia."

"Right." Alex nodded like it confirmed his thoughts. He pulled his smartphone out of his pocket. "Luckily we get internet access here but I suspect it won't be so easy on the yacht when they're travelling. Someone like Max needs to be in touch every day to keep tabs on an organisation of the size that he runs. He does have family involved, so someone on the plane today will be reporting to him."

"OK, that makes sense but I still don't see how it helps us."

He looked at her straitly. "We need to get our hands on his laptop, phone, tablet or whatever electronic device he's using to keep tabs on his business. We need his browser history and whatever is on his harddrive or cloud drive. But here's the trick - he can't know we've taken it. We'll have to ghost the whole thing and get it back before he knows it's gone."

Groaning, she dropped her head into her hands. "Seriously? I mean, even if we get it somehow, it's sure to be passworded. This is so... Mission Impossible. You can't really mean it?"

He gave her a wintry smile. "Feel free to tell me another way. This is the closest I've been able to get to him in four years. It's my only chance to get the information we need to put him away. You said you'd help. All I need you to do is get me into his room. Not everyone will have access to him and Amy. As maid of honour, you will."

"But *you* won't," she pointed out. "What excuse would there be for you being in his and Amy's rooms? Amy knows we only met yesterday and she'll have told Max. The whole Ebay thing was her idea in the first place!"

"Yes, Caz told me." He rubbed his face over with a hand again. "It could work to our advantage, though. From Caz's description, she strikes me as a bit of a romantic. Is she?"

"Oh yes." Kali rolled her eyes. "White knight, Cinderella syndrome to the hilt. That's why she likes Max - he rescued her. Swept her off her feet and took her away to the land of rich and famous she'd been trying to break into for years."

"Good. That means my idea should work." He grimaced, humour dancing in his eyes once again. "But you probably won't like it."

"Why?" She leaned back, suspicious.

"Because it involves me touching you - a lot."
*****

"So tell me everything!" Amy dragged Kali down onto an enormous curved couch and handed her a full glass of champagne. "Cheers." She clinked her glass against Kali's and took a sip.

Thunder rolled outside.

By the time Amy had called again to say she was free, the afternoon storm was already whipping across the island. Kali drove the short distance between their villas but still arrived wind-tossed and damp from the first drizzles of rain. Now it pounded against the windows, deafening.

Kali swallowed a mouthful, gaining a little time. It was too sweet for her taste. She surveyed the bridal suite. Enormous and luxurious were too mild a description of the rooms. They dwarfed an average suburban house. Three families could live comfortably here and hardly see each other. Pink marble, gilt, white silk and satin predominated, making it seem exotic and out of place in the tropical setting.

Amy wore an elegant, tailored white linen pants suit and a, low-cut red blouse to match her pouting red lips. Her normally-curly golden-blond hair was swept up into a smooth, straight pony tail. Blue eyes sparkled, their colour enhanced by the contacts that had long ago replaced the novelty glasses. Everything about her screamed money, style and glamour.

"You're looking stunning and umm..." Kali wagged a fingertip at Amy's prominent cleavage, "larger than when I saw you last. Fallen for the seductive lure of the plastic surgeon?"

Amy rolled her eyes. "As if. So not my style, no matter what the tabloids say." She plumped her breasts and grinned wickedly. "Just better lingerie with more...'padding' than I could ever afford before." She winked and Kali laughed.

When they'd travelled together as teenagers, Amy always stitched a few spare emergency dollars into the lining of her bra. They'd never needed it, but Amy claimed it made her feel more secure to know it was there. Sounded like she hadn't changed in that respect, anyway.

Speaking of her security blanket...

"Where is Max, anyway?" Kali craned to see if he was in the adjoining bedroom.

"Oh," Amy waved an airy, red-nailed hand, "he's still at his brother's villa. They had some business or other to catch up on. Won't be back for ages yet."

It clearly wouldn't be easy to isolate Max from his tech. If he was catching up on business, he'd have his computer with him, so no luck. Well, at least she could sound Amy out on the drugs issue. Question was: how to do it without arousing suspicion?

"Bummer, I haven't seen him for ages. How are you guys going?" Kali inspected her friend. She looked ok - a little thinner but her perfect makeup hid any signs of drug-use, if there were any.

"Oh, we're great." Amy sipped at her champagne. "He travels a lot, of course, but I'm so busy with auditions and everything that it's ok. Oh! I got a part in the new Bond movie!"

"Wow! That's so cool. What is it?" She had no difficulty imagining Amy in that sort of glamorous role.

Amy pouted a little. "Not the major Bond girl unfortunately, just a smaller role. I get killed off halfway through - of course! Still, it's better than porn or cancelled sitcoms." She sighed. "Being big in Australia doesn't necessarily mean big in the USA. It's harder than I thought to break in over there."

"What's it like socially? Are they nice to you?" Amy would have to change; become harder to get ahead in the States. She was beautiful and smarter than people thought but too tenderhearted to last long in what sounded like a cutthroat industry.

Amy screwed up her nose. "It's ok. They all like Aussies but there's a lot of competition, too."

"What about the drug scene you hear so much about?

Is it all over the place like they say?" Kali couldn't help glancing at Amy's arms, hidden by the long sleeves of her light jacket.

Amy laughed wholeheartedly, throwing her head back. "You sound just like Max. That was his one big rule - if I do drugs it's all over. I'm not that stupid. I like Max and he looks after me."

Kali had to bite her lip not to ask if she knew about Max's business. She still only had Alex's word for all this. She made a mental note to make that call to Castor as soon as she could, just to double check the whole story.

She tilted her head. "You 'like' Max? Don't you love him?"

The gorgeous blonde curled a lip and shrugged. "Sweetie I learned long ago that love is for idealists. In my industry there's no guarantees, so money wins over love. Max is good to me and he supports my acting. I don't have to wait tables or go the casting couch route so what the hell?"

"Wow," Kali blinked at her friend, "here I was thinking you were too softhearted to make it in Hollywood, Ames. What happened? You used to cry over dead birds and fall for every muso that crossed your path."

"Partly it was what happened to you. I realised that I needed to toughen up or I was going to get my heart broken and I don't want my career to be dependent on whether I'm sobbing my heart out and too miserably lovesick to go to auditions."

"Well," Kali said acerbically, "thanks for that masterly summation of my behaviour. I *am* tough, thank you!"

"Sweetie," Amy patted Kali's knee, "you come across all toughass but you've always been way more idealistic at heart than me - which is weird, because you're also such a cynic. I *know* romance is for fairytales, not real life. Rick really did a number on you and you weren't expecting it. You learned from it and, thank god, so did I."

Kali held up a hand. "Let's not go there. I have moved on, I promise Rick doesn't even cross my mind these days," she lied.

"Fair enough. Speaking of moving on - what's your Ebay guy like? Is he cute?" Amy giggled. "I can't wait to meet him!"

"Oh my God!" She summoned whatever acting ability she possessed and launched into the plan Alex had concocted. "He is unbelievably hot! When I first met him I was still angry with Caz for setting it up, so I hardly took any notice. But now! Whooo hooo!" She fanned herself. "And he's just so... so...." she sighed and stared dreamily out the window, "I don't know. Amazing. He's smart, and funny and incredibly talented. He likes all the same books and movies and music I do. I know it's only been half a day but he seems pretty...wonderful."

Had she overdone it? Amy gaped at her in astonishment. Then she reached out, tears in her eyes, and gave Kali a huge hug.

"Oh, Kali, I'm so glad." She carefully wiped her eyes with a finger tipped in scarlet and diamantes. "I know I said romance was for fairy tales but I was starting to worry that you'd never find anyone and you deserve someone better than Rick. I'm so happy for you!"

Chapter Six

"Hang on!" Kali held up a hand. "Don't jump the gun here. I said I like him and he's hot, not that I'm in love with him or anything!"

Amy gave her a knowing smirk but forbore to comment. "Well, let's just see how it goes then, shall we?" She squeezed Kali's hand. "We might have to arrange a few romantic getaways for you both while you're here."

"No! Don't be silly." Kali feigned a cross between hope and disregard. "I'm here to spend time with you and Max, not some guy I just met. I hardly know him. He can look after himself for a few days."

Amy wagged an admonishing finger. "Nope, that is just not good enough. I'm not letting you throw away your first real potential love interest in years like that. Of course I want to spend time with you though... I know! If we bring Alex along to whatever you and I are doing, then Max won't be able to complain he and I aren't spending time together and he'll have someone to talk to as well - so that solves that!" She leaned forward and whispered conspiratorially, even though they were alone. "He can get so jealous if I spend time with other people, poor lonely darling. I don't know what he did before he met me."

Satisfied with the results of her play-acting, Kali demurred again for appearances sake, which made Amy all the more determined to bring the four together as often as possible.

"In fact," Amy tapped her on the arm, "we'll start with breakfast tomorrow. Tonight's the rehearsal dinner, so we can't do much now, but we'll all get together here for breakfast at nine tomorrow. Does that suit you?"

"Sure, sounds good." Kali checked out the window. Palm leaves waved like flailing arms. The rain was almost horizontal. "It's almost three. Are you going to be able to hold the rehearsal on the beach at four if this storm keeps up?"

Amy screwed up her nose at the weather. "Well, we'll just have to have it in the ballroom instead but that was the contingency anyway."

Kali threw back the last of her champagne. "I guess I should go get changed - although I'll be soaked through no matter what I wear. How formal are we going for this?"

With a wave of her glass, Amy managed to indicate both that it didn't matter and that she would be stunning so whatever anyone else wore would pale into insignificance anyway. She giggled and Kali laughed with her.

Kali put the flute down and gave her friend a kiss and a hug. "I'll see you in the ballroom then at four. Is it just the bridal party to start with?"

"Yes," Amy smiled, "but bring Alex so we can introduce him to Max and he can watch the rehearsal. Maybe it will give him ideas."

*****

Kali left the suite with mixed feelings. Amy had definitely changed in the last year. Hard to say if that was Hollywood's influence or Max's. If she knew about Max's drug business it could explain the air of...brittleness about her. Or it could be just the stress of the wedding and the fact that she was obviously marrying for money rather than love. That was a bit of a shock. Amy had always been the soft, romantic-hearted one. She'd fallen in and out of love more often than Kali had changed shoes. Now, suddenly she was miss tough-as-nails mercenary? Weird.

She shoved open the downstairs glass doors of the bridal villa. Dashing through the blinding, torrential downpour, she reached the golf cart and managed to get back to the villa without crashing into anything. She scrambled to the door, shivering, soaked through, her green tshirt and white shorts clinging uncomfortably to her skin. At the front door she discovered she'd forgotten a keycard and knocked loudly. Would Alex even hear it over the howling wind and occasional thunderclap? After two knocks, the door flew open and he ushered her inside.

He wrapped her in the largest, fluffiest, whitest towel she'd ever seen and swept her off her feet, carrying her into the ensuite, ignoring her protests that she was perfectly capable of walking. Depositing her on the white-tiled floor, he scowled at her bedraggled state.

"I shouldn't have let you go out in this."

Kali pushed him aside, shivered and shoved wet hair back. "You have no bloody say in what I do or where I go. So back off."

He raised startled brows at her and offered a stiff apology, drawing himself up and stepping back.

She sighed, letting the overreaction go. It wasn't his fault. He hadn't really done anything wrong, apart from being a little over-protective.

"Sorry. But it wasn't dropping swimming pools from the sky when I left. Besides, it's only water. I won't melt. I'm just cold, which is ridiculous when you consider where we are. Get out so I can get warm."

He relaxed. Laughter lit his eyes for a moment. "Ten minutes or I'm coming back in to hear what happened."

"Oh, shut up." She closed the door.

She stripped, dropping her wet clothes on the floor, and stepped into the shower, increasing the heat until the room filled with steam and her skin tingled.

"So?" Alex's voice came from behind the frosted glass

divider.

She jumped, squeaked and stuck her head around the glass.

"What the hell are you doing in here? Stalking much?" She wiped water from her face.

He shrugged, leaned against the dual-sink, grey marble vanity and folded his arms.

"Ten minutes is up. You're taking too long and I wanted to know what happened with Amy."

"Out!" She pointed at the door.

"You may as well tell me. I can't see anything and I'm not going anywhere until you do." His smile shifted to gentle irony. "You're not in any danger from me, Kali, even apart from the fact that Castor would have my head if I hurt you. The fact is, you've got the rehearsal in under an hour, which means you'll be distracted by getting ready and I won't get any details from you."

"OK! OK." Kali laughed ruefully. "Point taken: I forgot to tell you. It worked. Amy thinks you're my newest, greatest love interest and she's insisting that you be included with the bridal party rehearsal so you can meet Max. You'll have to get dressed too."

"See?   That was important.   And excellent. Thankyou." He looked down at the floor for a moment, his face unreadable.

After a few moments of ongoing silence, she resigned herself and went back to showering. Only a doorless, semi-opaque sheet of glass separated them. If he took two steps to his right he would be able to see everything. Her nipples peaked.

"What else did she say?" His voice floated over.

Stoically ignoring the insistent throb of her body, she rinsed shampoo out of her hair and massaged conditioner in. Then she scrubbed her skin; probably with a little more force than necessary. It didn't help.

"She's certainly not marrying him for love but she

seems ok with that. She also said he won't hear of her doing drugs. Their relationship would be over if she did. Since she's basically marrying him for the money, I'd say she won't risk it. Still doesn't tell me if she knows what he does, though. Sorry."

"How did she seem, generally?"

The warm water slipped sensually over her skin. She slid her hands along the length of her hair, squeezing out the last of the conditioner as she considered Amy.

"She's definitely become harder in the last twelve months. She's on edge but I don't know if it's because she's working in Hollywood, stressed with the wedding planning or something else. I just didn't get the opportunity to ask without it seeming odd." She turned the water off and poked her head around the glass again. "Sorry. I'll try again tomorrow, I promise. I'm coming out now, can you go please?"

Alex stilled, holding their connection for a fraction longer than was comfortable. His gaze flicked down then jumped back to her face. He cleared his throat and turned away. Was there just the slightest flush of colour in his cheeks?

Kali looked down and gasped. Her mouth went dry, her heart thumped against her ribs. The glass frosting was a token. In reality it was practically transparent, showing every curve, every shape, every colour. She retreated into the shower space.

"Go!"

There was a moment of silence, then a single footstep on tiles and the sound of the door closing. She released the breath she'd held and poked her head cautiously out. He'd left. Something suspiciously like disappointment curdled in her belly. She let it go. There was too much weird stuff going on here. This was not the time to complicate matters with sex, especially since Alex was... well, no, the Google images had been made up, hadn't they?

Damn - it was all too foggy. She needed to talk to Castor.

She dried her hair then crept into the bedroom, swathed in towels. Alex was nowhere in sight and the door was closed. With a sigh of relief, or possibly regret, she sat on the enormous bed and pulled out her phone. A quick call to Castor confirmed Alex's horror story, plus some details he'd left out that brought a slow burn of anger and pity to her gut. Castor confirmed, too that Max was definitely connected and definitely the person of interest. He warned her that she and Alex were just there to gather information, nothing else.

"What the hell else would I do, Caz?" she demanded. "I'm not the secret squirrel. And why aren't you here? I don't believe that stupid excuse of not blowing your cover."

There was a long pause at the other end of the phone. Had the signal had dropped out?

"Caz?"

He groaned. "If you must know, and I'm surprised you haven't guessed since you're so damned good at seeing what you're not supposed to, it's Amy."

"Amy," Kali repeated, not understanding. Then several tiny clues over many years clicked together. "Amy? You liked her back in high school but I thought you were well over that. Still?"

"Still," he confirmed. "Don't tell her. I can't watch her marry someone else - especially someone like Max Chang."

"Why the hell don't you come here and tell her who he is?" It made no sense to her for Castor to let the woman he supposedly loved marry someone else, especially someone he knew to be scum of the Earth evil.

"Leave it, Kali, ok? I tried to tell her when they first got together but she wouldn't listen and without definitive proof I couldn't make her believe. Now my bosses here have vetoed my involvement because I'm too close to it. She's got the life she wanted, and, even once Chang is out of her life, she'll just find someone else who can give her that life. I can't, so just leave it." An uncharacteristic layer of steel in Castor's voice surprised her.

She blinked, unable to think of a reply. The two were well-suited but with Amy so fixated on the fast life Castor's choice to let her go made a stupid sort of sense.

"Just help Alex out and come home and we'll talk then, ok? Bye." He hung up before she could protest.

She sat for several minutes on the bed, phone in hand, staring blankly out the window. The rain died to a light drizzle and sunshine snuck through gaps in the clouds, making watery little rainbows and luminescent green patches on the tossed grey ocean.

Eventually she got up, selected a newly-pressed forest green cocktail dress from the pathetic selection hanging forlornly in one corner of the wardrobe and laid it out on the bed. It didn't take long to get ready, for she was methodical and simple in her routines. Three forty-five saw her twirling in front of the full length mirror, inspecting her reflection critically.

The dress still fit. She resolutely pushed aside memories of the last time she'd worn it and focussed instead on the now.

It swished elegantly around her knees, falling from a high waistline that emphasised her narrow waist and showed her moderate bust to its best advantage. Beaded straps framed a sweetheart neckline and clipped behind her neck, leaving her back bare. She pulled her long, dark hair up in a simple knot and left just a few long strands to curl onto her shoulders. With her fringe swept across to one side, tiny diamond drop earrings, and understated evening makeup, the look she'd gone for was retro-elegance. Whether she'd achieved it was debatable.

Meh. She shrugged at her reflection. It would do,

anyway. There was no point in competing with people like Amy, who lived in a world where beauty was a full time obsession.

Outside, the worst of the storm had finally blown itself out and the rain eased to a drizzle. The first hints of what would be a spectacular tropical sunset dusted golds and reds onto the remaining clouds. She was hugely tempted to just ditch the whole evening and take her camera to the beach to capture the spectacle. Unzipping her case she touched the camera and admired again the stunning colours as they softened the afternoon to blush pinks and greys. Zipping the case closed with a sigh, she picked up silver high heels and a matching evening bag in one hand, smoothed the other down the front of her dress, took a deep breath and opened the door to the living area.

It was empty. Alex was not there. She padded to the glass doors and peered out onto the verandah. Not there either. Repressing a spurt of annoyed disappointment, she reached for the house phone. A folded piece of paper addressed to her rested beside it.

I've gone to check out the area. Meet you at the ballroom at four. Jason will come and give you a lift if you call him.

A

She screwed it up and tossed it toward the wastebasket, missing. She dialled their young butler, strapped on her shoes and waited for him to arrive. He came. She greeted him as cheerfully as she could and waved him off when he deposited her out front of the function venue. Another, equally goodlooking, teenager opened the door for her and waved her in with instructions to head right and follow the signs.

Inside the blessedly-airconditioned building, she followed a babble of voices, one of which was distinctly Amy's, until she found the ballroom.

"There you are!" Amy hurried over, sashaying

elegantly in a fitted watered-silk cocktail dress of the most delicious shade of turquoise blue. "You look gorgeous, sweetie. Always loved that colour on you. Come and meet the rest of the crew." She took Kali by the hand and dragged her over to a small knot of men and women in one corner.

"Kalisa." Max took her hand from Amy and leaned in for a kiss, his dark eyes gleaming.

He, out of everyone she knew, called her by her full name. Maybe that's what unsettled her about him? He laid a hand on her shoulder and she flinched. No, it wasn't that. It was his habit of touching her. Never anywhere unacceptable, just that he always stood a little too close and touched a little too often. Personal space differed in different cultures, so she normally tolerated it, but after Alex's story he felt much to close for comfort. She edged away.

"So nice to see you again, Max. Thankyou for inviting me and paying for such a lovely resort."

He waved her thanks aside. "No, no. It's my pleasure. Nothing but the best for Amy. Now where is this young man of yours that she's been telling me about?"

"I'm here." Alex's deep, calm voice sounded just behind her shoulder.

Kali turned, inexplicably relieved to see him standing there. He wore a dark grey suit of impeccable cut over a crisp white shirt. In deference to the tropical setting he'd left the collar unbuttoned and was without a tie, but still managed to be the sharpest, hottest guy in the room.

She shook herself. Role-play; only pretend. She held out a hand to him.

He took it and moved closer, kissing her on the cheek and whispering into her ear at the same time, "You look absolutely incredible."

Her cheeks flushed hot and a genuine smile curved her lips as he pulled back and gazed down at her, his eyes warm. His hand curled, intertwining her fingers with his own.

Max cleared his throat and Kali started. She performed the introductions and stepped back half a pace to let Alex do his thing. He kept hold of her hand, pulling her gently back to his side. Max glanced back and forth between them, his eyes narrowing briefly.

It was impossible not to compare the two men: Alex, tall, lean, insanely handsome, gravely polite; Max slightly older, slightly shorter, starting to thicken a little around the waist and with a broad face, small hands, and a habit of sweeping one over his slick, black hair.

Alex appeared to have himself under control behind a mask of social politeness. Max also seemed at ease. He and Alex chatted amicably enough for awhile. Kali said little, not wanting to disrupt whatever plan Alex had for the conversation. If he had one, she couldn't tell. They spoke of little beyond the weather, the island and the upcoming wedding, but the tightness of his grip on her fingers betrayed Alex's inner tension.

The event co-ordinator called the bridal party to order and the rehearsal began. Alex lifted her hand to his lips in old-fashioned courtesy, flicked a warning glance at her and sauntered off to watch from a padded bench placed along the wall.

The whole wedding rehearsal wound up in a matter of thirty minutes. Kali and the three other bridesmaids, all but one girls Amy had known most of her life, stepped into their places opposite the four groomsmen. Kali arranged an invisible train and accepted an invisible bouquet. The celebrant blah-blah-blahed for a few minutes, Max and Amy pretended to exchange rings, kissed to the ribald amusement of all; then it was over bar the singing and throwing of confetti.

"Right!" Amy clapped, drawing everyone's attention. "Now for the fun part. All the other guests are coming to dinner in the reception hall next door in about half an hour, so let's go get the champagne started before they arrive."

Released from duty, Kali met Alex as he rose from the bench, glad again of his presence. There was something... comforting in having him around when she was in proximity to Max. She caught the trend of her thoughts and ground her teeth together. She did not need a man around to protect her from anyone. The last six years of her life had been dedicated to making sure of that.

"Did I tell you that you are breathtakingly beautiful?" Alex laid his palms on her shoulders and slid them slowly down her arms, catching her hands in his own.

The rest of the bridal party still milled about, chattering and laughing, somewhere behind, their presence colouring her response to his touch. Part of her couldn't help enjoying the compliment but the cynical part reminded her he just intended to prove the truth of their cover story.

"Thanks," she replied, avoiding meeting his eyes. "So what's the plan now?"

"Kali-"

"Oh my God, is that you, Alex?" A breathy, feminine voice behind made Kali glance over her shoulder in surprise. The fourth bridesmaid, the only one Kali didn't know, almost sprinted toward them. A stunning redhead, she was petite, with alabaster skin, cute pixie-cut hair and a figure to die for. Kali had already admired the woman's shimmering, silvery sheath-dress and killer heels. Now she homed in on Alex, radiating utter delight.

Chapter Seven

"It *is* you! It's Alex Schiffer. Don't you remember me? Lacey Hewitt." She laid a hand on her breast and actually fluttered her eyes winsomely. "We met last year in LA at the Lucasfilm Christmas party. We had *such* a nice time." She kissed Alex on the cheek and feathered a mischievous wink at Kali at the same time.

"Of course I remember, Lacey," Alex replied, ever-calm. "Let me introduce you to Kalisa. Kali, Lacey; Lacey, Kali. Kali is my date, so behave yourself Lace."

Lacey embraced Kali in a waft of expensive scent. "You're a lucky guy, Alex, she's gorgeous." Lacey linked an arm with each of them and dragged them toward the dining room. "Now you must tell me all about how you met. Amy said you bought Kali on *Ebay?* Is that even legal?"

"Funny," Kali sent an ironic look at Alex, "that was my question too."

A horrifying surge of what could only be labelled jealousy stewed in her guts. A large part of her desperately wanted to get the hell out, while another part wanted to stay and claw Lacey's expressive blue eyes out. Luckily, yet another part watched from a distance and commented that Lacey actually seemed quite nice, Alex didn't seem at all interested in her and that Kali herself needed to get a grip and stop letting other people control her emotions.

She stifled a giggle and dropped her head to hide it from the others. Voices in her head. Honestly.

But they were right: she could choose to let other people control her or she could choose to control her own emotions. Reactions she couldn't help. Actions and thoughts after that, she could.

She lifted her head. Alex watched her, one eyebrow raised in question. She sent him a half-smile. He disengaged from Lacey and caught Kali's hand, his faint smile warming just for a moment.

The three of them joined the rest of the bridal party at a large central table. Alex demurred and would have sat elsewhere but both Amy and Lacey insisted an extra chair be placed next to Kali's, so he joined them. The only downside, from Kali's point of view, was that, although Alex sat on her right, Max was on her left and Amy beyond him. Lacey sat to Alex's right and showed a tendency to monopolise him in conversation. That left her to talk with Max.

As the rest of the wedding guests filed into the dining room and took their seats, Max edged closer and laid a hand over hers, on the table. She managed to stop herself snatching it free. He leaned in, his breath fluttering a loose curl of her hair.

"I'm so glad you were able to get here, Kalisa. It means so much to both of us." He squeezed her hand gently.

Now how did she retrieve her hand without breaking his finger?

"And I see that Alex has found a friend. How nice." He leaned forward and studied Alex and Lacey, seeming just a little amused at their quiet interaction.

Kali resisted the urge to check. "Yes, evidently they met in LA last year at a party. How does Amy know Lacey?"

He squeezed her hand again and let it go to pick up his

glass of champagne. "Don't worry. You outshine her. I believe they are working together on the next Bond movie and have become quite close. I've been away on business a lot the last three months so I haven't met her until today." He glanced again at Alex and laid a hand on her shoulder. "I'm sure there's nothing for you to worry about."

She held herself rigidly still, as he caressed her shoulder, and tried not to show relief when he removed his hand and signalled for more champagne. She shifted as far away as possible but the chairs were packed in so it didn't really help. Under the table, a warm hand came to rest on her right leg. She jumped then released the quick-held breath.

It was Alex. He was engaged in conversation with Lacey but must have felt her move away from Max. Grateful, she put her hand on his and squeezed before shifting it off her leg. He reversed his hand in hers and clasped her fingers, not releasing them. He tugged her hand over and held it captive, his thumb brushing across the backs of her fingers in a highly distracting way. She was left in the awkward position of having only one hand free and being obliged to drink with her left.

How long was long enough before it was polite to reclaim her hand? Alex's light strokes sent tingling spikes of desire right to her core.

A few seconds later she was rescued by the arrival of the entree. Hers turned out to be the lamb, a meat of which she was not particularly fond. Max and Alex both had something interesting in chicken. She picked up her fork, prodding the lamb without enthusiasm. A second later, the plate vanished, to be replaced by the chicken dish. Beside her, Alex was already cutting into the lamb he'd swapped. When she exclaimed he leaned over and murmured.

"You didn't look very impressed. Besides, it's good for our image. Isn't it what all good dates do for their girl?"

Kali bit back a caustic reply. "Thanks. Are you enjoying catching up with Lacey?"

He leaned a little closer, lowering his voice. "You don't need to be jealous, you know."

Glaring at him, she turned back to her plate, not dignifying his comment with an answer. His warm fingers caught her chin and tilted her face toward him. His grey eyes searched hers intently.

"I mean it," he whispered, kissing her swiftly on the mouth.

She caught her breath at the flood of heat washing through her body. Every sense came alive; every inch of heated skin hot ached for his touch; every nerve fluttered, attuned to his proximity. For a moment, she leaned into it, responding, revelling in the sense of connection, desire and in the warmth of his lips and hand. It had been so long since she'd allowed herself to feel this way.

Laughter swept through the room. She jerked back, pressing her fingers to her mouth. Alex looked a question at her, silently asking what was wrong. She shook her head, trying to dispel the connection. It was all an act for Max and Amy's benefit, she had to remember that. She put a forkful of chicken into her mouth, chewing without tasting it.

Beside her, Max leaned over again, his lips brushing her ear as he murmured into it. "It would seem that Alex is a very lucky man."

She flinched then controlled it and managed a smile. He put an arm around her shoulders and, at the same time, around Amy's and squeezed both women.

"I'm a lucky man, too." He kissed Amy's forehead and she leaned into him.

Kali jumped as his fingers edged a little too low and brushed the side of her breast. Her internal tension level ramped up. She'd never been comfortable with casual contact the way Max was. It was all too much: the last day, Alex, Max and Amy, this whole ridiculous scenario. Things were happening too fast. She needed time and space to process everything; to work out what was important; to get her head straight.

Pushing back her chair, she dropped her napkin on to it and picked up her purse. Amy and Max looked up at her in surprise.

"I'm just going to... y'know," she lied.

Amy pointed to one of the exits.

It took all of her self-control to walk there, head high, shoulders back, and not run like a child escaping a threat.

*****

Once outside, she leaned against a cool wall for a second and regrouped. She just needed a little time to think and a roomful of partying people wasn't the best place to do that. She'd never been a huge party-person anyway. That was Amy and Castor's scene. She was always the one to sit in a corner and watch, or talk with one or two interesting people, rather than flirting and winning over everyone. So nobody would really miss her if she didn't go back, would they? Well, Alex might but if they all thought she was in the ladies it would take awhile anyway.

So she bypassed the bathroom and headed out the door to the beach.

At almost six o'clock the sun wasn't fully set. The last rays still lit scattered clouds in the west with a glorious array of orange, pink and grey. In the east the first hints of nighttime purple coloured the horizon, blending sky with sea in a sweep of colour that would make artists reach for their cameras or brushes.

Kali was in no mood to appreciate it. She pulled off her highheeled sandals and hooked them through the strap of her bag, slinging both over one shoulder. Beneath her feet, gravel gave way to fine white sand that squeaked as she walked. Still faintly warm from the day and still damp from rain, it clung to her feet and got between her toes.

She strolled down to the waters' edge. Waves sloshed and retreated gently, small and calm again after the storm. Low tide left a vast expanse of beach exposed: half darkened and smoothed by the waves, half white and mounded by walkers. Hers were the only footprints on the smooth area and it gave her pleasure to be alone on the beach.

It stretched for quite a distance in both directions and from here the villas and buildings were barely visible. There rose a comforting sensation of being alone on a deserted island – exactly what she wanted at this moment.

For ages she simply stood and gazed out to sea, allowing the wash and backwash of the waves to exercise a soothing effect on her stretched nerves. She breathed deeply the salt-scented, clean air and let the breath out in a long, slow sigh of contentment. A wave slipped over her feet, cooling heated skin, drawing out the stress of the day.

A hand gripped her right shoulder. She reacted. She grabbed the hand with her left and backed under her attacker's arm. A deft twist applied a wrist lock. Dropping her right forearm into his bent elbow she drove his head toward the ground.

Gasping, she let go at the last second.

He stumbled, recovered and stood up, shaking his wrist, apparently unfazed.

"Alex." Her voice trembled with the beat of her heart. "Please don't do that again."

"No," he replied, faintly admiring, "I won't. Nice move by the way. Where'd you learn it?"

She ignored the question. "Look, I don't feel like being with lots of people at the moment. I did my bit. You've met Max, you've got Lacey to keep you entertained. Can you just leave me alone for a little while?"

"Is that what's bothering you? Lacey?" He stepped toward her and stopped as she backed a step away. Shaking his head he shoved his hands into his pockets. "I told you, you don't have to worry about her. She's not an old girlfriend or anything. She's with Caz's office. I've never met her before. She's an IT expert operating undercover in LA and posing as an actress to get to know Amy. Caz sent her to help once we get the computer, that's all."

Kali strode up the beach toward their villa, hating the fact that the news affected her; relieved her of jealousy. Sand scrunched behind her. She swung around, one hand out.

"Just leave me alone, ok?"

Alex stopped a few feet away, keeping his hands behind him, calmly inquiring. "Why? Talk to me."

She backed up a few more steps. "If you've got Lacey, then get her to help you get the computer. You don't need me. Just move in with her and let me be."

"If I could, I would, believe me," he replied. "I don't want you to be in this position at all but I don't have any other options." He moved closer, reaching out then dropping his hand when she twitched away.

"Why not? Lacey is more qualified than me and she knows Amy pretty well by the looks of it," she argued, trying to ignore the empathy in him that invited her to confide. "I'm not some sort of super-spy. I can't do this. I'm sorry to let you down." She backed up, his proximity too disturbing to be borne at the moment.

Alex regarded her solemnly, his hands now fisted by his sides. He shoved them back into his pockets, the action serving to emphasise the breadth of his shoulders. Kali looked away, pulling a strand of hair from her lips as the salt-breeze fluttered it. All around them, the evening darkened and stars prickled the purpling sky.

He drew a deep breath. "Kali, Max doesn't want Lacey, he wants you. She won't be able to get close to him; to distract him. You will." His tone was flat, almost angry, his face cold and distant.

She gasped, bile rising as the import of his words hit home. She wrapped her arms around herself, staring out at the silvertipped ocean.

"No. No, he doesn't. He wants Amy. He's marrying Amy."

Alex gripped her shoulders, gently, compelling her to face him; and the truth. "C'mon, Kali. You said it yourself. He makes you uncomfortable. You just didn't want to see it. I could see it after ten seconds. Yes, he's marrying Amy but he *wants* you."

"Fine," she snapped, shoving his hands away, resenting him for making her admit what she didn't want to. "I know it, ok. I've always known it. Happy? Is that what you want me to do? You want me to seduce him and keep him occupied so you can copy his harddrive?" She glared at him, breathing hard and trying not to choke up on her own past; her own fears; her own hurt. "I will *not* let a man use me that way. I will not sleep with someone - not Max, not anyone - for any reason but my own. Ever. So just back off Alex. Use someone else. Leave me alone."

She took a few more steps away, holding tears down by force of will.

"This isn't about Max, is it?" His soft question stopped her. "Or me."

Kali turned her back on him and started up the beach again. He caught up with her and strode silently alongside.

"Go away, Alex."

"Not until you tell me what's going on," he replied, apparently undisturbed by her angry outburst. "Then I'll leave you completely alone - if that's what you want me to do."

She stopped in her tracks and glowered at him. "So, if I just tell you why I can't do it, you won't make me? How will you get the computer?"

He smiled twistedly at her. "First of all I don't think anyone could *make* you do anything and I never intended to anyway. I'll work something else out. I'm resourceful and I've worked a long time to get here but I won't put anyone else in danger to achieve my ends. Mental or physical danger. Just tell me why this bothers you so much - apart from the fact that Max is a sleazebag and you obviously have good taste. I want to understand."

"Why?" Suspicious, she pressed her lips together. "So you can work out how to fix me and manipulate me into doing what you need?"

"Stop it!" Alex's sharp tone brought her spiralling hurt and fear up short. More than a hint of anger clouded his face. "Stop it. You're seeing things in my actions that just aren't there. I'm not out to force you or manipulate you to do anything you don't want to. Get that into your head and we can move on. I..." He stopped, took a deep breath and continued, "I just want to understand why you're so afraid."

He was right. She groaned, all the fight seeping away like water into sand. She was using anger as a shield, acting on baseless beliefs and old programming - exactly what she'd been trying to train herself out of for years. With a heavy sigh she climbed the wooden stairs onto their villa verandah and pulled a keycard out of her purse. She dusted the sand off her feet as best she could and led the way inside. Alex pulled the door closed and flicked on the lights and airconditioning, shutting out insects and the warm, heavy night air.

Kali tossed her shoes and purse onto a side table and leaned her hands on the cold stone kitchen counter, her back to him. She couldn't meet his eyes. This was hard enough. She drew a deep breath, trying to steady her heart and relax her throat so she could talk. Even Amy only knew some of the story; Castor barely any. This would be the first time in six years she'd told anyone.

Would unburdening her soul make her feel better, or just dredge up old memories to besmirch her hard-won self-belief? Either way, it looked like the only way to get Alex to back off was to tell him the truth. He would either leave her alone out of pity and disgust or he would leave her alone at her request. At least he would stop the games, hopefully.

"I came to university in Brisbane when I was eighteen," she began quietly. "Amy went to NIDA acting school and Caz went to Sydney University, so my two best friends weren't with me. Don't get me wrong," she caught Alex's reflection in the glass splashback and smiled faintly at him, "I had a great time for the first three years. I learned to party and drink, had a couple of boyfriends - two good, one not so good - all the usual things kids get up to at university I suppose."

She moved to sit on the arm of a couch, poised to get out if things turned ugly, opposite where Alex sat. Picking up a cushion she held it on her lap, wrapping her arms around it.

"Then, when I was just about finished my degree, one of my friends introduced me to someone new; five years older; rich; sophisticated: Rick Bowman." She clutched the pillow closer. "We dated for a few weeks and he turned my head with his money, his smooth chivalry, his ultimate gentleman routine. I was going through a phase of enjoying being... pretty...and making the most of it."

She huffed a scornful laugh and shook her head. "Anyway I got a lot of attention, so I had no trouble believing him. Then, when uni was over and I had to move out of my sharehouse and get a job, he offered his spare room to me. It was like a dream come true. He was everything a young, stupid, naive girl dreams of - handsome, rich, cultured, well-travelled." She grimaced bitterly. "It never occurred to me to ask why someone like that would want an inexperienced, immature girl. I just thought he loved me."

She paused. How much more should she say? Alex

shifted from his couch to hers, watching her without expression. He opened his mouth.

"No," she waved a hand at him, "don't say anything, please. Let me finish. You have no idea how hard this is." She blew out a breath and continued. "Rick...well, he was good at what he did. It took me a year to realise how much I'd changed; how much he'd messed with my head. He had this incredible, subtle way of implying that anything I did wasn't quite right; wasn't quite as good as it could've been - as it would've been if I'd done it his way instead. He behaved like a spoiled, self-centred only child, even though he mentioned having a brother. It's funny," she cast Alex a wintry smile, "you'd think having a sibling would ground someone, but he was amazingly insecure."

Alex looked down, saying nothing.

Kali gave a sour laugh. "Of course I was desperate to have his approval; not to disappoint him. It was a downward spiral. I believed him - he was so much more experienced and I've always been good a doubting myself, so I took what he said on board and internalised it. Before long it wasn't just daily tasks and decisions and thinking he was changing; it was how I dressed, what I would do for a job; how much I saw my friends and family; what happened to my money. He took everything from me. .Lived off my earnings." She shivered again, closing her eyes against the memories. "And when he got angry at me that was somehow my fault as well. He made it sound like he was the victim."

"Toward the end, I would've done...did do almost anything he asked. It was... humiliating, but I did it because he'd twisted my head so much that I thought it was normal; ok; expected. I thought I wasn't wise enough to make my own decisions; that I couldn't survive without him; that it was me who was the problem. He just wanted a slave, basically; someone to worship him; someone he could control."

She gave a rueful laugh and plucked at the gauzy skirt of her dress. "Hell, last time I wore this we got into a fight because I'd spoken to someone he didn't want me to. I asked him why he was so rude to me." Her mouth twisted. "He said it was because I deserved it."

Chapter Eight

Alex made a hasty, uncontrolled movement with one hand. She jumped and gripped the cushion tighter against her stomach, averting her face. He stilled. There was a long silence.

"How did you get out?" His soft question jerked her out of unprofitable memories.

She threw the cushion aside, stood up, then sat straight back down, composing herself with an effort.

"One day I made him so angry..." she paused and groaned, covering her eyes for a second and drawing a long breath. "No, he *got* so angry at me that he hit me. Just once; a slap." She touched her cheek, the tiny, white scar there. "The ring on his finger drew blood."

Beside her, Alex tensed, growling, low and deep in his throat. At least he restrained himself and didn't say anything.

Kali rose to pace the room restlessly, twining a long curl of hair around her finger.

"He told me it was my own fault and stormed out. A few minutes later, I found myself curled up on the floor, crying, begging him not to leave. Suddenly I saw everything I'd become and everything he'd done to me quite clearly for what they were: lies and manipulations based in his own insecurities. It was like waking up from a long coma. I was myself again." She scraped her fingers through her hair. "It didn't last long - just long enough for me to pack my bags and get out. After that it was six months of fighting with myself before I stopped thinking I should go back and a year before I stopped wondering if he missed me and looking for his car as I drove around."

She laughed grimly. "I couldn't even talk to anyone. None of my friends believed me. All they saw was the charm of him. They couldn't comprehend abuse that wasn't physical and obvious. His friends all though he was a great guy. I felt like an idiot, anyway, so it was safer not to say anything."

She sat down on the couch again, facing Alex, determined. "It's taken me years. Years to get back the self-confidence he stripped away from me. I've had just two other boyfriends and neither lasted more than a few months. Every man I meet who's interested in me wants something from me; wants to change me. I just can't risk losing myself again. I'll change myself because I want to grow and get better but I won't let anyone else dictate who I should be."

Tentatively, she put a hand on his arm. It tensed beneath her touch. "I knew from the start you had an agenda. No one buys a girl for that much money and expects nothing back. I figured it couldn't be sex, not with all those women on Google. So it had to be something specific about coming here, to this wedding. So I watched you. I saw when you tried to divert my questions. I knew you were using me for something."

His jaw worked but his grey eyes never left hers.

She took her hand away. "Please understand. I want to help Amy, and you, but I'm too...broken. I can't trust anyone yet and what you're asking of me," she swept a hand around at the villa, the island, "I'm not sure I can do it and stay whole. Max makes me feel just like Rick did - dirty; sick. I'm a little afraid of him and I don't trust him. It's like he's hiding some big secret and is just...I don't know." She shook her head, unable to put into words exactly what made her uneasy about Max.

Studying Alex, she was struck again by his quiet strength and masculinity; the beautiful tension in him that made him both attractive and enigmatic.

"Then there's you, Alex."

He blinked, a flicker of something like surprise showing for a moment before the controlled himself again. He had amazing self-control. She leaned closer, touching his fabulous mouth with her fingertips. He sucked a quick breath and froze, his body tensing.

"With you it's different. I also can't help that I find you incredibly sexy. You turn me on so fast it's frightening. I go to jelly when you touch me and that scares me. With you I feel like I'm totally out of control; like I'd do anything to have you - and that's doubly scary. With you, I can't trust myself."

An incongruously cheerful rock song interrupted the uncomfortable silence. Kali blinked in confusion. Oh. It was her mobile phone ringtone for Amy. She fumbled in her tiny evening bag.

"Hi Amy, sorry, I'm just not feeling one hundred percent. Alex took me home."

"Oh," Amy sounded disappointed, her voice blurred, "here I was hoping he'd taken you away to have wild passionate sex with you. "

Kali avoided Alex's questioning look. "No. What's happening tomorrow?"

"Well, I'll get the kitchen to send your dinner over instead. Tomorrow's pretty relaxed. There are still a few stragglers coming in and Max has business meetings all day, so I haven't planned anything major except the boys are having their buck's night of course. Waterskiing and go-karting and stuff for you! Oh, and my mum's coming in so I'll spend the evening with her. Remember breakfast, though." She giggled. "I'll get you two into bed together yet."

She sounded fairly smashed. No point in arguing with her, she probably wouldn't remember anyway.

"Sure, Ames. See you then…at breakfast, I mean," Kali agreed and signed off. She set the phone down and pulled enough courage up to meet Alex's eye.

"We're supposed to go to breakfast with them at nine tomorrow." She waved a hand at the phone. "What do you want to do?"

He sucked a sudden, sharp breath, his expression harder and bleaker than she had yet seen it.

"I think, first of all, I should apologise." He stretched out a hand then stopped and let it fall to his lap. "Then I should go back to the mainland and let you be." He got up, picked his jacket up and draped it over his arm. "I'll ask Jason to find me another room somewhere tonight. You take the bed. I'm sorry I put you through this, Kali." He headed toward the bedroom.

She jumped up off the couch, unaccountably distressed. "No! I didn't mean for that. I don't want you to lose all you've worked for, Alex. I..." she gripped his wrist, "I just wanted you to stop-"

"What?" He swung around. "Stop what? No, it doesn't matter. If my being here is causing you that much pain, then I won't stay. I won't be responsible for hurting you any more." With that, he spun away and strode into the bedroom, leaving Kali gaping after him.

She ran to the bedroom door. His suitcase lay on the bed. He flung clothes into it with an air of barely-restrained anger.

"Alex, I don't understand."

His expression hardened for a moment. "No, I know you don't." He stalked into the bathroom and returned with his toiletries bag in hand.

"You can't go!" She grabbed a handful of his clothes and threw them back toward the wardrobe.

He watched them fall, walked over, picked them up and put them back in without comment.

She reached over and closed the lid with a snap. "Alex, you can't give up on what you're here to do because I have issues. I can't let my best friend marry someone like Max and you're the best hope we have of stopping him."

Alex rested his hands on the bed, dropping his head down. Running a hand through his hair he shoved it into disarray as he sank onto the bed. She pushed his case aside and sat beside him. He immediately stood and paced the room in a display of restlessness that seemed uncharacteristic. Long strides took him across the room and back. Every time he passed her his scowl deepened. Eventually he slowed and finally stopped and faced her, hands deep in his pockets, calmer but still with hints of some darker emotion she didn't understand.

"Alright." He nodded shortly. "I agree that we can't let Amy marry him and I agree that this is probably my only opportunity to get the information we need to put him away. However that means I now have two agendas and I'm damned if I can think of a way to achieve both of them without putting you into a situation you're not comfortable with and not trained for."

"I know." She sighed. "I think that realisation, back at dinner, is what brought this all to a head. The look in Max's eyes, the way he touched me..." She grimaced and drew a deep breath, wiping damp palms on the skirt of her dress. "I know what I have to do. I just don't want to do it. Not only because of him and my history, but because I'll lose Amy as well."

She wrapped her arms around her waist and stared at her bare, sandy feet. The silence was broken only by the soft wash and crash of waves on the beach, and the eerie wailing cry of curlew night-birds.

"No," he growled, "there's got to be another way. We're just not thinking straight."

"We both know there isn't, but if it makes you feel better," she gave a wry shrug, "I'd be happy if you thought of one."

"Believe me," he gave a bitter laugh, "I'll be happy, too. You've no idea how."

Before she could ask what he meant, he extended a hand to her, his harsh expression softening to understanding. "Look, we've had a long day and we missed dinner. Let's get some room service and sleep on it. I'll take the couch."

"Amy's sending dinner over, so that's taken care of," Kali managed a laugh. She took his hand and he pulled her to her feet. "And the bed...I thought you were so unchivalrous when you didn't offer before."

Alex stepped a little closer. "I thought you were a tough woman who needed to prove her equality to herself and to me. So which are you - the equal or the princess in need of rescuing?"

A long, tense silence stretched between them. Shoving aside her initial, annoyed reaction, she gave a shaky laugh, stepping back to put much-needed space between them.

She tucked a loose hair behind her ear. "You know, I'm not really sure. I think I've spent years proving I'm tough and independent but, when you think about it, having to prove it means I'm still searching for outside approval and recognition of the fact. So maybe, deep down, I'm still hoping someone will rescue me. Pathetic, huh?" She sneered at her own stupidity.

He laughed softly and walked over to the fishtank, leaning his broad shoulders on the wall and apparently studying the fish with great interest. "No, I think we all want to be rescued sometimes."

"Even you?" Kali blinked at him, incredulous. "You seem so...cool, calm and collected all the time."

"Ha, yes, now." Reflected in the glass, his smile held a whisper of sadness. "That's taken work. In the first year after I lost Michelle and Jack I just wanted someone to make it all un-happen, if you know what I mean. After that, I was like you," he came back and took her hand, drawing her toward the front room, "needing to prove that I could tough it out; that I could handle it all on my own."

He took her other hand, his thumbs sweeping distractingly across the backs of her hands.

"Now," he leaned in, his eyes falling to her mouth, "I think-"

A knock at the front door made them both jump. Alex gave a rueful chuckle and went to answer it. The ever-cheerful Jason strolled in bearing silver-domed platters and a bottle of wine. Kali used the opportunity to go to the bathroom and fix her makeup. In the other room, Alex dismissed Jason for the night

"Smells good. Hungry?" he called out.

She took a deep breath and came out of the bedroom, having regained some equanimity in his brief absence. Pouring her history out seemed a little overdramatic now. In all honesty, it wasn't even that bad compared to some people's lives and it didn't bother her often any more. It was just the current situation and the intensity of the chemistry between her and Alex that stirred it all up.

What her reaction did prove, was that she hadn't gotten over it. She'd just suppressed some of the insecurities under fierce independence and a feverish need to control her life; proving instead that Rick still controlled her in some small way. Every time she felt the need to control the situation or another person, she let him call the shots.

True security was in accepting that most things were out of her control. Then in making the right choices for herself in every situation, based on *her* priorities and values. Making the small, everyday choices that would get her one step closer to her dreams and goals - not choosing as a reaction against something that happened years before.

Fear of falling back into one trap had simply led her

into a different one.

Pausing at the bedroom door, she looked at Alex anew. He was focussed on setting the food out, hands busy, sensuous mouth relaxed, profile calm again. He dominated the room with his presence, yet made no effort to be larger than life - he just was. It was natural for him to lead but he didn't need to control or belittle and therein lay the biggest difference between him and Rick.

He glanced up. "You still look beautiful but also hungry. Come and eat. No lamb this time. Would you prefer the chicken or the fish?" He gestured at the table.

"How about we go halves?" She slid into a chair and picked up a knife and fork. He agreed, opened a bottle of sauvignon blanc and poured them both a half-glass before sitting down.

They ate dinner in companionable silence, with no need to fill the gaps with unnecessary talk. For Kali, it was the most comfortable she'd felt with him so far; as though her openness had created a tentative trust between them that hadn't existed prior. For some reason, that made her nervous all over again. He seemed perfectly at ease.

Setting her wine glass down, she checked the clock. Only seven o'clock. Restless again, she cleared away the dishes. She poured a third glass of wine, then hesitated and put it aside, taking up water instead. Two glasses of alcohol and she felt a little lightheaded. Clearly out of practice.

Taking her glass, she wandered over to the balcony doors and stared out into the darkness. There wasn't much to see with the lights on behind her - a couple of faint glimmers from a boat moored well off-shore, a row of dim, low level solar garden lights to show the way to the beach for those inclined to take night time walks. She wasn't really paying attention anyway. At last, decided, she turned to find Alex reclined on a couch, watching her gravely.

She swallowed the last mouthful of water and twirled

the glass between her fingers, one arm folded across her waist. It was time. She needed to do the right thing, as hard as it might be.

"I'll do it." The words didn't come easily, accompanied as they were by mental images of what they might mean for her.

"What?" He drained his glass and set it aside, impassive. Rising, he stood before her, took her glass from her fingers and put it down.

Kali wrapped both arms across herself and focussed on the centre of his chest.

"I'll do what I have to, to help you get that computer but," she swallowed hard, "we both know I'll have to get into Max's room - or better yet, get him out of it so you can get in there." She tried to be dispassionate about it. "The smartest way would be for me to get him out so you and Lacey can do what you need to without fear of being interrupted. If I can do it in such a way that it will also discourage Amy from marrying him, then so much the better."

He took her hands in his and unpeeled them from her waist. She turned her face aside.

"We don't have to do it that way," he said. "We can just wait until he goes out on one of the organised events."

"No, that won't work." She looked quickly at him and away again. "He has security shadowing him and his brother is in business with him, so he would leave his computer with one of them if he knew he was going out. It has to be... unexpected and with a short timeframe - twenty to thirty minutes maximum - so he won't feel insecure about leaving it. We can't risk involving Amy, either, because we don't know if she's in with him or not. She may not want to sacrifice what she's got."

"Kali," he rubbed his thumbs across the backs of her hands, "don't make decisions now. Sleep on it and we're sure to come up with another idea. We have until

Thursday, after all."

"No, we don't." She pulled her hands free, folding her arms and walking away a few steps. "We have until Wednesday night. The best chance will be that night, since the Bucks night is tomorrow and I won't be able to get out of the Hens night on Monday or the Masquerade on Tuesday and there's other organised events through the days."

He moved up behind her. The warmth of his hands fell on her shoulders. If only she could lean into him, lean on him, have him make all this go away. No. That was dependent-thinking. Amy was her friend to protect, not his.

"As I said," his breath stirred the loose curls of hair brushing her neck, "sleep on it."

"Alright," she agreed, moving away, suddenly unnerved by his closeness. There was too much attraction between them. It clouded her thinking. Had she agreed just to help Amy or because she wanted to please Alex? It was a slippery slope and she had to be careful or she'd get suckered straight back down into self-oblivion again.

He waved a hand at the couch. "Relax. I'll make you tea, then we can…you can go to bed. Now's not the time to think too hard about it. We can still come up with an alternative."

"No. I..." she paused, tucking a strand of hair behind her ear and checking the time. It was only seven thirty. Too early to go to bed and she couldn't bear lying there on her own, thinking about Max, with Alex in the next room. Nor was she yet ready to take any next steps with him. The situation was too tense. Chemistry there was, but there had to be more than chemistry for her to risk herself again.

"I think I'll go for a walk on the beach." She headed for the bedroom.

"Want company?"

He eyed her shrewdly, with a hint of concern, hands tucked into his armpits as he leaned casually against the wall. She shook her head.

"I'll change and get out of your hair for awhile. I just need some space. I'll be ok." She closed the bedroom door behind her and leaned against it.   She definitely needed time to think.

Shucking her dress, she changed into a loose tshirt and light linen pants, and slipped out of the bedroom door that opened straight onto the balcony. As she passed the living room doors, she glanced up to find him watching her levelly through the glass door. He turned away.

Chapter Nine

She ran to the beach, revelling in the soft humidity of the cooling night air, the squeak and crunch of soft sand, blue-white in the moonlight, the taste of salt and freedom. The tide edged back in; gentle waves creeping slowly up the beach. A shimmering path of moonlight flickered and danced over the tiny breakers, inviting would be swimmers into calm tropical waters. She briefly regretted not changing into bathers and headed north to walk slowly in parallel with the lapping waves, their rhythmic swish and wash soothing her troubled thoughts.

After a hundred or so steps, she angled up the beach a little and brushed aside the top layer of damp sand to find a dry patch beneath. She sat, staring vacantly out at the full moon. Picking out a stick and a shell from under her backside, she shifted to get comfortable and leaned back on her elbows.

The stars glittered overhead, a sparkling sweep across an unpolluted sky. The last few flickers of lightning flashed off to the south as the storm headed toward the mainland and left the island in humid peace. The quiet-dark lent perspective to the world and serenity seeped into her soul. It had been a long and disturbing day. She needed time out to think, time away from people, time to work out truth from fiction, her own fears from reality.

Lying flat, Kali let her eyelids drift closed and relaxed

at last. She drew long, deep breaths of cool, damp night air and released tension with every exhalation. Crickets and frogs chirruped softly nearby. The wail of a curlew sent a pleasurable shiver down her spine. She stroked the damp sand and rubbed the grains between her fingertips, focussing on the feel of the tiny grains against her skin, letting stress and worry go.

A soft scrunching and faint vibration through the sand alerted her that someone else walked the beach. She opened her eyes a crack. Maybe if she stayed still the newcomer wouldn't even see her and would walk right by. No such luck. Whoever it was, he headed directly toward her, his face moon-shadowed.

She recognised his walk and sat up in a hurry, scrambling to her feet as he came within earshot. Something primal in her did not want to be caught lying down in his proximity. All the anxiety surged back, hammering heart against lungs and stealing breath.

"Max." She busied herself dusting sand off her pants. "What're you doing here? Is the party over already? Where's Amy?"

"Amy's having fun with her girlfriends." He stopped just a little too close. "I needed some air."

She clamped down on the instinctive urge to back away and held her ground.

"Well," she said cheerfully, wishing for some way to let Alex know he was here, "I'll leave you to it. I'm about to head back to the cabin. I guess I'll see you guys at breakfast."

This was the prime moment to set up a clandestine meeting with him at some other time - a time when Alex would have a chance to getting into his room and his hardware. Unfortunately, Kali could not for the life of her think of any reason why, given the suggestion, the clandestine meeting shouldn't be here and now. If she went down that path right now, there was no benefit in it.

There was no way of letting Alex know. Somehow, she had to tread a fine line between showing enough interest to string Max along and not so much that he tried something at this moment.

"Kalisa?" His soft, questioning use of her name made her look at him inquiringly. He gazed back at her for a long time, eyes dark and thoughtful.

"Yes?" she finally prompted, her sense of unease ramping up. "I'd best get back. I told Alex I'd only be ten minutes."

Max frowned, his lips thinning into displeasure. "Of course," he began, then paused and laid a hand on her arm.

Her skin goosepimpled at his touch. It was a huge effort not to shake it free and run like hell.

"If you have a moment this week, perhaps when there's no events planned," he tilted his head at her, "could we have a drink together? I have... a proposition for you."

"Oh?" She blinked at him, unable to believe he'd just offered exactly the opportunity she needed. Hiding a shiver of disgust, she shrugged. "Sure. Amy's got my number. Text me yours and I'll buzz you when I've got a free moment. Sounds...intriguing." She attempted to give him a slightly puzzled, slightly interested and slightly flirtatious look. "Anyway, I'd best get back. I'm due to call my family in about ten minutes as well. Night Max."

"Ah yes, your brother, Castor isn't it? Wish him well for me. Amy has told me much about him. It was...unfortunate he couldn't come. Goodnight Kalisa." He inclined his head, watching as she strode away.

She walked steadily. Her legs itched to run. Her heart urged it. She kept to a fast walk, head high, arms swinging like someone with nothing to worry about.

She reached the villa at long last and slid the glass door closed behind her with a relieved sigh. She locked it, taking satisfaction in the solid click of the mechanism.

"That was quick. Something wrong?"

She jumped, hand flying to chest in reaction to Alex's deep voice. He stuck his head out of the bedroom door, his hair wet, shoulders and neck bare. Obviously straight from the shower. She swallowed. Was he naked?

"All fine. I just ran into Max and didn't want to stay on the beach alone with him." She drew nervous fingers through the windblown length of her hair. "You know."

Alex stepped into the lounge. She gulped and looked resolutely away. He wore only a towel, wrapped around his narrow hips, his chest bare, muscular, smooth and tanned. Apparently unaware of the effect he had on her heart rate, he reached her in five long strides and gripped her arms painfully.

"You ok?" His frown deepened.

"Sure." She twisted free and moved toward the kitchen, pouring a cold glass of water. Anything to douse the heat in her belly. "It was just frustrating because I had no way of letting you know that he was with me. Would've been a prime opportunity to get into his room. I'll have to get your mobile number."

"Mmmmm." He shook his head. "No, you were right: any times when there are planned events won't work. His computer wouldn't be accessible now anyway. Lacey just called. She's been chatting with Amy and confirmed what we suspected. Their room has keycoded security and four guards - two inside and two outside - any time Max and Amy aren't in the room. They only send the guards out when they're in the room themselves.

"No," he paced lightly over to stand opposite her across the kitchen island bench, "I think you're right. We're out of options. As much as I hate to do it to you, I think our only chance is when Max is out with you but Amy is in by herself. Somehow I'll have to distract Amy enough to get Lacey into the bedroom, where I assume he'll keep the laptop or whatever, then get Amy to where you are in order to complete the scene."

She shivered at the image of that 'scene'. "Well, Max says he has a proposition for me and he wants to get together to discuss it. I told him I'd call when I had time free. Sounds like that might be our best opportunity."

"Yes," he agreed, watching her solemnly.

There was a long, awkward silence. She fiddled with her water glass, chewing on the end of a lock of hair, as she had when she was a child. She caught herself and spat it out.

"I guess I'd better get to bed." She walked out from behind the bench. "Goodnight then."

Alex lifted a hand as she walked by, then dropped it back to his side, his expression hooded. "'Night, Kali. Sleep well."

At the doorway, she looked back at him, only to find he'd moved to the verandah door and stood with his back to her. His reflection in the glass showed only his usual, calm visage. So why did she get the feeling he was angry?

*****

She rose late the next day, surprised at how long and how well she'd slept, considering the turmoil of the previous day. The clock showed seven-thirty. Time for a swim. She tied her hair roughly up in a pony tail and changed into her one piece bathers. Grabbing a towel, she slid quietly out the external bedroom door and ran down to the waters' edge. Dropping the towel she eased into the glassy surface, enjoying the cool smoothness of the salt water.

The sun shimmered a hand or two above the horizon, its heat warming the day already, its brilliance glittering a thousand reflections off the calm ocean. She swam parallel to the beach in one direction for ten minutes, then flipped and swam back, her strokes smooth and easy. Swimming was cathartic. It freed her mind to ramble as her body went on automatic and brought the day on in a relaxed, invigorating style unlike any other type of exercise.

Her cabin came up onshore. She slowed and dropped her feet to the sandy bottom. She pulled the hairtie out and rose from the water, sweeping hair from her eyes and rubbing salt water away. The silence, freedom and stillness of this place appealed deeply to her and she drew a deep, contented breath of clean air.

"Not a bad view."

A deep voice behind made her spin. From the beach, Alex eyed her with wry amusement. He was bare to the waist, clad only in blue board shorts, his golden skin glowing in the early light.

"If you like ridiculously picture perfect tropical beach settings, I suppose." She smiled back, keeping her eyes fixed on his.

He waded into the water until he reached hip height, then dove beneath its glittering skin. He emerged a few feet away, shaking water from his hair, only to dive back under again. This time he stayed down so long she grew concerned. Then a slight ripple and a push of water around her legs gave warning and she didn't jump when he appeared right in front of her. He eased himself up through the smooth water, rising like a mythical merman, his skin warm and gleaming in the morning light, hair darkened and slick, fingers rubbing his eyes clear as he stood, broad shoulders blocking the sun.

"I don't think I've seen you so relaxed and happy," he said. "You like swimming."

Kali lifted a shoulder. "Sure. It's...meditative. Like doing a good workout at the dojo, you know. Focusses you on the here and now."

The sun slanted through his eyes, catching yellow glints in the grey. "Dojo huh? I figured you'd had some training after you put that sweet lock on me last night. How long?"

She swished her hands through the glittering, rippling waves. How much was it safe to reveal? Her sensei always said to keep her training to herself. But she'd already given it away so... "About ten years all up. Four or five years when we were teenagers but then I stopped. Took it up again after I left Rick. Helped me get my confidence back."

Alex moved closer, reaching out and pushing a wayward, wet curl out off her cheek. "Yes," he murmured, "I understand...and I'm sorry."

She screwed her nose up at him. "What do you have to be sorry about? It wasn't your fault I fell for a manipulative, abusive bastard."

Looking down at her with a somewhat enigmatic expression, he laid his hands on her collarbones and put his thumbs under her chin. She stood still but brought her hands to rest on his forearms, ready to push him aside if need be. She definitely wasn't ready to dive into anything other than the ocean right now. The situation was difficult enough without complicating it by taking their attraction any further.

"We're being watched," he murmured, lowering his head slowly toward her. His grip tightened as she automatically turned to check. "Don't look. He's up the beach about fifty metres behind you."

"So if you want me to seduce him," Kali muttered, trying to ignore the fluttering of her heart, "surely pretending we're an item is going to make that tricky. If he thinks I'm falling for you, what excuse will I have for seducing him?"

"Somehow," he paused, searching her face closely, "I think you know you're not going to have to even try. He's the sort to want what he can't have and he's not the sort to wait for a come on. We'll make sure you're not alone with him long and I'm glad to know you've had self-defence training. Think you can handle him?"

She gripped his wrists tighter as the implication of what he said sank in. She swallowed then nodded hesitantly. "Yes, but I don't know if he'll come through undamaged."

"That...would not be a bad thing." He pressed his lips together for a moment, his eyes glittering like the sea. "Now we need to give him a bit of a show to heighten his...desire to possess you." Before she could react, he relaxed into a smile and kissed her, gently and without emotion.

It was bizarre.

Considering the chemistry between them and how unbelievably passionate his kisses had been yesterday, the lack of feeling was disconcerting. He seemed to have some sort of internal switch to turn sex on and off at will. What sort of man could do that? A man with a serious goal and singleminded focus on it. A man whose focus was elsewhere and who just used the tools he needed to in order to achieve the ends he wanted. It was a chilling realisation.

Mindful of their audience, she slid her hands up his arms and looped them around his shoulders, pressing herself against his body as though in abandoned pleasure. His fingers slipped down the length of her back, down to her backside, caressing, kneading, stroking. After that first, brief, kiss, he moved his mouth to her cheek and now began murmuring instructions into her ear.

"He's still watching. I'm going to ramp things up. Can you run with it?"

When she breathlessly agreed, he slid his hands back up to her shoulders. Her one-piece was decorative, not a proper pair of racing bathers. The straps slid easily off her shoulders. From a watcher's point of view, it would appear as though she was bared to the waist, in full view of the world. In reality, Alex carefully pressed her body close against his, trapping the material in place over her breasts. Kali threw her head back and moaned aloud as he kissed her neck and nibbled her ear.

"Right," he whispered at last, "someone else is coming

up the beach. Max is walking away. We're good."

She checked behind. He was right. Max's stocky form disappeared over the crest of the dune. Something in her stomach relaxed, just a fraction.

Alex slid the straps back into place and took a half pace back, his expression faintly worried.

"You ok?"

She struggled for control. He might be unaffected but her body responded to his touch - the scent and warmth of his skin; the feel of his lips on hers - even against her best efforts.

She nodded. "Of course. It's just..." She paused and sucked a deep breath to try and calm her racing heart. "As you said, I'm not really trained for this. It's hard to stay...detached like you do."

"Yes," he replied, turning away, "it is." Wading back toward shore, he called over his shoulder. "Breakfast is in an hour. Do you want to shower first?"

"Sure." She pushed through the water, glad to find her knees weren't shaking too badly. My God, if he ever really directed the full force of his sexuality on her, she wasn't at all sure she could resist.

Unfortunately, she was now quite sure that she should. How could any woman ever believe he actually cared for her? He was too cool; too calculating. He used sex as a weapon in a way that she'd never thought possible in men. Women were often accused of using sex to get what they wanted; of being able to feign attraction and arousal. Clearly men could do the same. Alex had it down to a fine art. He switched it on and off at will without it ever coming near his heart.

A man like that was dangerous.

Chapter Ten

An hour later a burly Malaysian security guard scrutinised them closely as he opened the door to the Bridal suite.

"Amy," Kali embraced and inspected her friend, "you seem a little worse for wear. Late night?"

Amy groaned and shaded her bloodshot eyes with one perfectly manicured hand. "Don't remind me. I don't think breakfast was such a good idea any more. Not sure I can stomach bacon and eggs. Max darling, Kali and Alex are here."

Max came out of the bedroom, still in a white terry bathrobe, towelling his hair dry. At the sight of his slightly paunchy frame and broad face, Kali clenched her teeth. He shook hands with Alex, who responded with a calm greeting. Then, with a flickering glance at Kali, Alex turned his charm on Amy.

"Max." Kali forced a smile and bore a kiss on the cheek with equanimity. Beside her, Alex stiffened.

The four sat at a white and glass table, set for breakfast, on the balcony. The villa was tucked away on the mountainside, commanding a stunning view across the bay and out over the ocean. The beach was clearly visible. Max must have seen her swimming and come down deliberately. She clenched her fists and swallowed down a rush of saliva. How would she get through the next couple of days in his proximity? How could Amy stand him?

She laid her napkin across her lap, fussing with it as an excuse not to look at Max. She reached for a jug of icy orange juice and pretended not to watch Amy as she said blithely,

"So, Caz sent his best, Amy. Wished you both luck."

Amy jumped a little and cast a quick, narrow look across at her, then another at Max. Faint colour bloomed in her hangover-pale cheeks. Ah, so *that*'s how it was. Kali held her face still with an effort. How had she missed it all these years? Amy *did* care for Castor and Kali had just been too blind to notice.

Distracted, she ignored the somewhat stilted conversation about the weather going on between Alex and Max, thinking hard instead about how to get Amy and Castor together. If she could somehow bring that about, it was possible her friendship could be salvaged as well. Chewing her lower lip, she helped herself to bacon, eggs and toast served by Amy's inevitably-handsome young butler.

In a lull in the general conversation, she eyed the couple and asked with false cheer. "So what's the plan for today?"

Amy scowled at her. "Didn't we have that conversation last night?" She yawned. "I'm sure I remember asking you if you and Alex were having-"

"Dinner! Yes," she kicked Amy under the table, "but you sounded pretty wasted so I figured I'd double check. Don't want to miss anything important."

Amy glowered then giggled as Alex covered a cough that sounded suspiciously like a chuckle. Kali ignored him. Max sipped his coffee, apparently not following the unspoken part of the conversation. Kali silently gave thanks for English being his second language.

"Well, I'm busy this morning, so you get all the fun without me," Amy's smile soured, "but I know you. This resort is wasted on you. You'd prefer to be off by yourself taking photos of trees or bugs."

"Buildings, Ames," Kali said patiently. "I'm a commercial photographer, remember? Architecture, that sort of thing?"

"Boring and safe. You were better at photographing people until Ri-" Catching Kali's warning glare, she dismissed her profession with a wave of a manicured hand and brightened. "I've just remembered: all the girls in the bridal party have a final fitting today at three. We had to change the dresses a bit and the dressmaker wants to be sure no-one's gained weight. She's an artiste dahling!" She wrinkled her perfect nose. "So we're all getting together for afternoon drinks here first at two-thirty. Other than that, I'm pretty much spending the day sorting out last minute issues and my agent is also flying in with some scripts I've got to read through and decide on before the end of the week."

With a blink of surprise, Kali swallowed a mouthful of juice. "Hasn't your agent heard of email and skype?"

Amy yawned and poured herself coffee. "He's invited to the wedding as well, so he figured he could bring them along. It just means I'll be tied up all day so we won't be able to catch up until tomorrow. That ok?"

Was Amy deliberately putting their catch up off? Did she suspect Max's attraction? Could a word or two now, before the wedding, save Amy a lot of pain later? No. That wouldn't be fair to Alex. He deserved closure. His family did. There was no other obvious way out of this. And Kali wasn't a good enough actress to hide her nervousness from Amy for long, so it was best not to spend too much time in her company, anyway.

"No problems." She took a bite of egg. "I'll just drag Alex around to all the adventure stuff I can find and we'll keep ourselves busy. Max," she turned an inquiring look to him, "are you busy too?"

For a moment, there was a flare of something...hunger

maybe... in his dark eyes before he inclined his head. "Unfortunately my brother brought several business matters to my attention that need to be dealt with. I'll be in conference all day but I'm anticipating catching up with everyone at the bachelor's party tonight." He bowed again, graciously, toward Alex this time. "I hope we can get to know each other better, Alex. I'm sure we have much in common. I hear you're quite the philanthropist." His smile was reminiscent and proud. "I like to think I provide services that help people, too. Perhaps we can even do business together."

Beside her, Alex tensed and Kali laid a hand on his knee. He lifted his coffee cup in salute and murmured a polite nothing, his jaw muscles working and eyes cold.

Amy picked at a croissant, tearing off tiny pieces and putting them between scarlet lips. "And tonight I'll be holed up here with my mother who will, undoubtedly, tell me how many mistakes I'm making in my life."

Kali chuckled. "I like your mum. She's good people. She always took in strays and waifs after school, like Caz and I."

She kept her hand on Alex's leg until she felt him relax back into his chair. Max seemed oblivious to his hostility.

"I know!" Amy rolled her eyes. "Our house was like Grand Central Station."

"Oh and you hated it," Kali teased. "Most of them were guys trying to impress you and your mum so they could ask you out on a date."

"My fans dahling, my fans." Amy laid a hand dramatically against her forehead.

Everyone laughed and applied themselves to finishing breakfast. Alex pushed his half-full plate aside.

After an interminable second coffee, Max excused himself and Amy made noises about having to get ready, so Kali and Alex left.

Outside, in the warm sun, she looked sideways at him.

He seemed unruffled.

"You ok?"

"Perfectly," he replied affably. "So?" He paused at the path to their cabin.

"So what?" She glanced up at him, confused. He obviously didn't want to talk about breakfast, so what was he on about?

He flashed a smile, white against his olive skin. "Seems we have a day free of espionage. What shall we do? What would you like to do? Day spa? Massage?"

She sent him a world-weary look. "Thanks, but that's more Amy's style. I was thinking more along the lines of go-karting and the rifle range or archery." She surveyed the skies. "And maybe, if it doesn't storm again, we could go scuba diving tomorrow. I've always wanted to."

"Really?" Now it was Alex's turn to raise his brows at her.

"Really," she affirmed. He could probably use the distraction, as much as she could. "Up for a bit of a competition today? Best of three?"

He chuckled. "Possibly, what are the stakes?"

Kali walked a few more steps. They reached their doorstep and he swiped the keycard. One hand on the open door, he paused, smiling down at her, head cocked in question. Heat flashed into her cheeks as the silence extended and the ever-simmering tension between them flared again.

"How about the bed?" he said, as she fought to think straight.

"W.what?" With her back pressed against the doorframe, she couldn't get any further away.

Sheer wickedness gleamed in his eyes for a nanosecond. "Whoever wins gets to sleep in the bed rather than the couch."

She sagged. Should she be relieved, disappointed or insulted? She managed a blasé shrug. "Sure, why not?"

They headed for the archery range first. It was outdoors and set on the side of a long, slightly sloping grassy hill. Overlooking the western side of the island, it encompassed beautiful views across the tossed teal ocean toward the mainland. Overhead gulls circled and called, brilliant white against a sharp blue sky. In the fringing rainforest, bright coloured parrots squawked, squabbled and flashed crimson against the green.

Kali climbed out of the golf cart and stood, hands on hips, surveying the landscape. The wind picked at her ponytail and tossed it into her face. She scraped it back and took a deep breath. The air tasted clean with a hint of damp earth and greenery. So much better than being in the city. In spite of the bizarre situation she was currently part of, relaxation seeped into her shoulders and she drew another long breath.

"Ready?" Alex's deep-voiced query brought her back to the moment and the excitement of anticipated competition fluttered in her belly.

She grinned over at him and the range instructor who appeared magically by his side. "Of course. My middle name is Robin Hood, well Marion maybe."

The instructor took them through obligatory safety protocols and fitted them with bows and arm and finger guards. She inspected the gear. This was none of your rubbishy cheap school-kid quality equipment. The bows were high-quality recurves of various sizes. She chose a twenty-five pound draw, knowing that she'd regret anything else tomorrow. The last time she'd played around with archery was at Uni and her muscles weren't used to it now. Standing up to the line, she drew the string back, anchored it, and let out a long, slow breath as she lined up the target. Allowing for the slight crosswind, she released the string and the arrow sailed away. It thunked satisfactorily into the target, just outside the second gold centre ring. She adjusted the sights a little.

"Close," Alex admired, "and not too bad for a first shot."

Stepping up to the line, he drew his bow with a smooth, relaxed motion that made her groan inside. He'd done this before, too. Sure enough, his arrow found its mark inside the second ring. He flashed a wicked little smirk that made her purse her lips.

Six ends of six shots later each and the range instructor called a halt to their competition. They'd agreed he would judge the results. Examining both their targets, he finished totalling and handed them both over.

"I'd have to say that Mr Schiffer wins this round, ma'am but only by a small margin. Sorry." He shrugged deprecatingly.

Kali laughed ruefully, scrutinising both fluttering bits of paper again. "No, you're right. He beat me fair and square."

"Next?" Alex raised an eyebrow at her.

"Sure, although I have a feeling you may take me on this one, too. Let's go for the rifle range. If we do go-karting first my hands will be too shaky to shoot straight."

"Competitive, are we?" His rare smile flashed.

She put her nose in the air. "Just don't want to sleep on the couch, thanks."

They drove to the rifle and pistol shooting range and pulled up on the gravel drive out front of the main building. There were several different indoor ranges and a couple of outdoor ones. Between two of the buildings nestled a small cafe, aptly named 'Hunters' Hide', built in an airconditioned glass and polished timber style that would have been at home in the middle of upmarket Sydney.

They entered the reception, got kitted out with earmuffs and given the safety talk by the instructor. After a short, amicable argument, they agreed on a mini-competition of three lots of ten shots - ten using a rifle with a telescopic sight, ten without, and ten with a pistol. The instructor offered to take their equipment to the first range and get it ready for them.

Strolling beside Alex, towards the indoor rifle range, Kali turned to him and slid an arm around his waist. She leaned her head on his shoulder and gazed up at him adoringly. After a moment's hesitation, he draped an arm around her, eyes wary and questioning.

"Kiss me," she whispered.

His eyes narrowed, flickered for a moment to take in their surroundings then, alight with understanding, came back to hers. Leaning down, he captured her mouth and drew her close against his body. This time she was prepared for it but the gentleness and skill of his kiss still took her breath away. His wandering hands came to rest on her hips and she jerked as his thumbs dug into the sensitive hollows there. Angling his head, he deepened the kiss, pulling them out of the pathway and into a cosy arbour tucked away from view of the glassed in cafe where Max sat in conference with his cronies.

Surprisingly, even when they were hidden, Alex didn't stop kissing her. Instead, he bit at her lower lip, his tongue sweeping across to soothe the pleasurable pain. His hands caught her head, fingers buried in her hair as he pulled her hairtie free and dragged at the silky lengths. With the faintest groan, he ran his hands once down the length of her back then circled her waist and pushed her away in a sudden move that left her dazed.

He closed his eyes and stayed perfectly still for a several seconds. Kali, breathing hard, watched him warily. At last, he straightened, apparently unaffected.

"We may have to rethink this."

Kali blinked at him, bewildered. "What, the random kissing? That's fine with me!" Her reply was more acerbic than she intended but he messed with her thinking and it was annoying to find him unruffled.

His jaw tensed then relaxed into his usual, calm. "No,

I mean the shooting. I'd rather not have Max see what either of us can do with a gun."

She folded her arms across her chest. "That good are you?"

He sent her that sexy half-smile. "Probably, and Caz tells me he trained you himself, but the main reason is that I don't want him thinking of us in those terms. I want him to consider both of us as harmless and seeing someone with a gun in their hands tends to make you reconsider the definition of 'harmless'."

"That's fair enough, I guess," she agreed. "We can come back..." she paused and laid a hand on his arm.

Footsteps sounded on the concrete path outside their hiding place. A voice spoke. With no time to warn Alex, she slid back into contact with him, caught his face in her hands and kissed him. He froze then, when she nipped at his lip and pressed against him, melted beneath her hands. His arms wrapped around her, cradling her close. His hands slipped beneath her shirt, caressing the skin of her back and stomach. His mouth on hers was warm, hungry, demanding, with an edge of passion that was missing before - as if she'd taken him unawares and he didn't quite have himself under control. What an interesting concept.

The footsteps and voices came close, passed and died away. With an effort, she disengaged herself before she lost it. Kissing Alex was far, far too addictive.

This time he scowled at her with something like anger snapping in his stormcloud eyes. "What the hell?"

"Max." She jerked her head sideways. "I heard him coming." She checked but he and his companion were out of sight. "He's gone and I don't think he recognised us if he saw us. He said something about a package being ready on Tuesday night for shipment to Thailand. Does that mean anything to you? Do you think it's important?" Glancing back at Alex she paused then cocked her head at him.

His expression shifted into a strange mix of surprise, frustration and amusement.

"What's so funny?" She put her hands on her hips and glared at him.

He shook his head and tugged at his collar. He picked up her hairtie from the floor and handed it to her.

"Nothing you've done," he assured her. "I'm laughing at myself."

"Why?" She couldn't help the edge of suspicion that crept into her tone.

"Because you never cease to surprise me and I should know better than to underestimate you by now. Of *course* you speak Mandarin." He chuckled.

"I had a Chinese flatmate at uni for three years," she said. "Chin Ling insisted we speak Mandarin at home. After she refused to pay her half the bills unless I asked her in Mandarin; and then started having long conversations with her girlfriends, while pointing and giggling at me, I realised I'd better learn fast."

Alex laughed, his face alight, joy lifting years of hurt from it. Kali smiled. That was the real Alex for the first time: alive, happy, relaxed; not shut down and hurting. This was how he should look; how he would have looked before he lost Michelle and Paul. She liked him this way and it fuelled her determination to see the whole thing through. She'd been self-centred and self-protective for a long time. Maybe it was time to help someone else.

His laugh faded into a wry grin and he tucked her hand into his. "C'mon, let's see if you shoot as well as you kiss."

Heat flushed into her cheeks and she pressed cool fingers to her cheekbones in a surreptitious attempt to push the colour back down. And once more he'd evaded her questions about Max's conversation. He really was irritating sometimes. This whole 'keep Kali in the dark' thing was long past being tiresome.

Chapter Eleven

Determined to beat him, she called up meditation techniques to steady her racing heart and shaking hands. She donned the earmuffs and checked the rifle before bringing it up to nestle in the crook of her shoulder. All her focus was on the target, on her breathing, on the tempting centre of those small, distant circles. Ignoring all the muffled sounds around: the curses of someone in the next booth who kept missing, the sharp report of Alex's rifle as he took his ten shots, the deep hum of airconditioners; she brought the twenty-two up to her shoulder and sank into it. Halfway through a slow exhale she held the breath and squeezed the trigger.

After checking, she reloaded, aimed, fired; reloaded, aimed, fired - ten times in methodical succession. Signalling the supervisor to switch her target, she ignored the white paper as it returned to her booth on a string pulley and was replaced with a fresh one. Accepting the rifle with no telescopic sight, she adjusted her vision to the gun, relaxed, breathed out and squeezed: bang. Reload; bang; Reload; bang. Ten times.

In the zone, she signalled again and picked up the pistol. Again the target swept in and back out again. This time it was a closer distance. Shifting her stance, she relaxed her shoulders, straightened her arms and squeezed - ten times in measured succession. Standing up straight, she ejected the magazine laid the pistol down with a nod to the supervisor. He drew her target in and handed all three to her with an encouraging thumbs up. Kali accepted them with a word of thanks, liking the clusters.

Alex waited nearby, holding his own in one hand, cool and unruffled as usual. Jerking his head back toward the cafe he slipped the earmuffs off and handed them to the supervisor. She did the same, rubbing her ears as the sound of gunfire thrummed against her eardrums.

Together they shoved through the doublethick glass cafe doors and into blessedly cool silence broken only by the tinkle of coffee cups and the murmur of voices. The smell of fresh coffee mingled with the scent of gunpowder still clinging to their clothes.

Finding a booth in a corner, she laid her papers down on the table and gave Alex a challenging grin.

"You add up mine and I'll do yours," she pushed them across and took his.

There followed silence awhile as they each totalled. Swapping numbers, she checked and re-totalled hers and his then sat back with a laugh.

"That's silly. How could we possibly have got exactly the same total?"

He shrugged. "We'll have to call it a draw. You had a great cluster with the pistol. Beat me by a mile there."

"I spent a lot of time on the range with Caz after…well…" She shrugged and pulled out his result for the rifles. "We were about even for the unsighted rifle but you pretty much blasted a bloody great hole in one spot with the telescopic sighted one. Practice much?"

For an instant, there was a flicker of cold, hard determination in those slate eyes and Kali binked at him. She leaned across the smooth timber tabletop, her hand on the target paper.

"Really? Your fallback position is to kill him sniper-style if you can't get him by legal means? That's what's in your other suitcase, isn't it? Are you serious?" She stared at him in disbelief. "You do still have something to lose, you know."

"No, I don't. I have no family left…of consequence." His reply was flat, his return look devoid of emotion, the line of his jaw sharpened by something unspoken.

"Oh." Impulsively, she reached across and took his hands in her own. "I guarantee, Alex, there are people who care about you and who would hate to see you in prison. It's not worth it. We'll get to him another way. Don't throw your life away, please?"

Something flashed behind the hardness in him; some other, unidentifiable, emotion. Had she got through to him? If nothing else, his intention made her own clearer: she had to help him get the evidence against Max. Hers wasn't much of a sacrifice, really, compared to what Alex was prepared to give up and she couldn't let him do that. He was worth it, that much was obvious. That small glimpse of the real man; his unexpected willingness to sacrifice his long term goal when she was made uncomfortable; it made her more determined to help free him from this burden of his past.

His expression softened into amusement and he drew his hands out from beneath hers. Picking up the menu he perused it with the calm, relaxed air of one who has said all he's going to say and revealed all he's going to reveal.

"Shall we get a coffee or lunch?"

She sat back. He was a hard case and she had no right to give him advice, he was just too polite to say so. She picked up the menu.

"Early lunch."

He signalled a waiter and ordered their food. She refused wine and stuck to juice.

"I need my wits about me for the go-karting," she said when he questioned her choice.

He smiled. "Fair enough, but we celebrate the winner

with a decent bottle of champagne this afternoon after your dress fitting."

"Deal." Kali clinked her glass against his.

Their meals came and they ate slowly, interspersed with easy chatter about work, movies and vague generalities about the upcoming wedding events, both avoiding any more painful topics by unspoken consent. Outside the tropical sun played hide and seek behind fluffy white clouds, cooling a sticky, warm day to at least bearable temperatures. At last, as they sipped coffees, Alex eyed her speculatively.

"So what are you going to do with yourself this evening when I'm out at the buck's party?" He put his cup down, grimacing. "Not that I particularly want to go."

"It would look suspicious if you didn't. I'll catch up on some work, check emails, that sort of thing. Why?"

"Just curious." He took another sip. "What do you do for fun?"

She laughed. "Today has been the most fun I've had for ages. I've spent the last three years getting my photography business off the ground and believe me, that's no fun at all. It's only the last two that I started making enough money to live on."

"Yes." He swirled the last of his coffee in the cup, his expression understanding. "It took me a couple years to get things moving, too. You're actually doing well if you're making a profit so soon. Means you're making a name and a service business like photography is all about connections. Let me know if you ever need any mentoring."

She tilted her head. "I thought you said you weren't a super-rich businessman. How much of the Google stuff was actually true?"

He chuckled and pushed his cup aside. "Not the women, certainly. I haven't had time for that sort of thing lately. I Googled you, too, you know. You do keep a low media profile, don't you? You don't even have a photo of yourself or your name on your business website. Why's that? It can't be good for business."

Kali drew abstract figures on the table with the condensation from her softdrink. She pursed her lips and shrugged. "I didn't want Rick to be able to find me so I've stayed off the grid as much as possible. It's not easy though. Most of my social media is under a fake name and limited to people who know me. It probably has slowed me down, I guess, but I feel safer."

He spun his coffee cup slowly on the table, his eyes clouded. Why? Any mention of Rick seemed to bother him. Was he just one of those overly-protective men or was there something else? Was he more affected by the chemistry between them than she thought? Jealousy?

Dismissing the idea as crazy, she gave him a wry grin. "I'm not that much into social stuff anyway, as you've probably worked out. I'm an action junkie but not much of a party person. I always left that up to Ames and Caz. He's mad and she's the most determined person I've ever met."

He slanted an amused look at her. "Caz talks about you often. He thinks very highly of you."

She snorted and almost choked on her drink. "Well, it would be nice if he told *me* occasionally." Dabbing at her mouth with the serviette gave her a chance to recover.

"I guess that's siblings for you - they don't always tell each other what they ought to." He glanced away, a frown flickering across his brow.

"Hey," she brushed her fingertips across the back of his hand, "I'm sure she knew you loved her."

The frown deepened then vanished as he composed himself. He smiled but there was more puzzlement than joy in it.

"You do have a remarkable knack for reading my thoughts, don't you? Am I that transparent?"

Blushing, Kali shook her head. "No, I've always been pretty good at reading people - most people that is." She shrugged it away, changing the subject. "So you never did tell me - if you're not a billionaire playboy businessman, what are you and where did you get the money for that stupid ebay stunt?"

His lids drooped, eyes sparkling with humour now. "Well, of course Castor helped out with the whole thing but I think the bidding went a little higher than even he expected. There was one guy in particular who kept outbidding us, right up to the last minute."

"Who was it?"

He gave her a wicked little smile. "No idea. Possibly just someone who fancied that photo."

She groaned and dropped her head into her hands. "I still can't believe he used that. But," she shoved stiff fingers through her hair, pushing it back. "I also don't get why Caz didn't just call me up and ask me to let you give me a lift?"

"That would've been our solution, if Amy hadn't come up with the Ebay idea." He tossed back the last of his drink. "The auction was a much better way of making my trip here seem unplanned and unsuspicious. Otherwise how would we have explained my sudden appearance in your life right when you needed someone with a plane?"

"I guess, it's just all a bit...convenient, don't you think?"

Alex paused, cocked his head and gazed off into space for a moment.

"No, there were at least five other people bidding and it was touch and go who would win, right up to the last. Caz's people weren't happy. They footed half the bill. I don't see how it could appear to be anything but what it was."

"What? Like some desperate girl hunting for a wealthy guy to fly her to an exclusive island wedding?" she said caustically.

He laughed. "More like a desperate guy buying time with a gorgeous woman."

"Oh please." She snorted a laugh. "After those shots on Google of you dripping models? Were they honestly all set up?"

His smile held secret humour. "I told you, yes, and Caz warned me you wouldn't take compliments."

"Did he now? It sounds to me like my little brother has been entirely too talkative for someone in the secret-keeping industry." She shoved away from the table. "Shall we go drive too fast and pretend to be James Bond some more?"

He stood as well, waving a hand magnanimously in the direction of the door. "After you ma'am."

They rode in silence to the go-kart track.

Why did she find it so hard to accept compliments? Somehow, a belief that she had to downplay all her achievements had crept into her thinking and she wasn't sure when or how. It was one thing to be modest but her thinking trended toward the 'not good enough'. She'd come to believe that nothing she did was quite enough; that no matter how hard she worked and how great the results, she could've done better. Where had that come from? She sighed. Bloody Rick again. Why the hell was she *still* letting that twerp control her life?

Angry with herself but wanting to concentrate, Kali shoved it aside for later and focussed on what lay in front of her right now. At the track, while Alex drove, she asked the instructor to point out the apex of each corner and listened carefully as he talked her through the course. It was a neat little course, full of tight turns. The smell of fuel and rubber seeped even into the airconditioned waiting room. Here, instead of an upmarket cafe, there was a little shop selling snacks and drinks, plus a room full of car video games. It had a more kid-friendly feel. How many celebrity kids had spent time here with their parents?

From a seat at a massive observation window overlooking the track, she saluted Alex and gave him a thumbs up when he squealed into the pit after his fifth lap. A check of his time on the board made her whistle. She'd have to be pretty damned quick to beat him. He entered the waiting room, grinning a challenge, slightly smug. She jammed her helmet on. Right. Game on.

It took two laps before she got a feel for the cart and started to hit the turns properly. By the time she headed into the fourth lap out of her allotted five, her cheeks hurt from grinning. The seatbelt clasp dug into her hip. Her fingers and forearms ached from gripping the wheel. The smell of hot rubber, petrol and warm tarmac fired her blood. She'd found all the sweet spots in the track. She was practically part of the zippy little cart beneath her. Inches from the ground, she threw the machine around the track, barely touching the brake, hitting each corner like a pro.

As she flew down the final straight and screeched to a halt, all of her angst had burned away with the rubber. Too little action and too much time to think, that was her problem. She'd always been bad at relaxing and doing nothing. Her laid back, funloving brother called her intense and restless. She needed to stop sitting around thinking too much.

Unbuckling, she yanked off her helmet and fluffed out her hair. The instructor appeared by the cart, beaming as he held out a hand to help her.

"Well done ma'am," he said. "You came within a second of the lap record and that was set by a professional driver."

Kali scrambled free of the machine and bounced into the waiting area inside the building.

Alex swept her an elaborate bow. "I concede that one to your superior driving." He headed toward the exit, smiling down at her as she floated beside him.

"I won?" She waved back over her shoulder at the instructor.

"Fair and square." Alex held the door for her. "And now I believe it's time I dropped you off for the more girly activity of drinking, giggling and trying on clothing."

That brought her down off the high with a thud. "Do I have to? This is much more fun."

He chuckled. "Caz was right. You are certainly an unusual woman, Kalisa Brooker."

"What?" She wrinkled her nose scornfully as he eased himself into the drivers' seat of the golf cart. She swung in beside him. "Because I can drive and shoot? Sexist are we? I'm sure I'm not the only woman who can. By the way, maybe I should drive from now on?"

"If you want, I don't mind. As long as you don't take the corners like it's a go-kart." With a sidelong glance across at her, he turned the key. "I'm curious though, why can you drive and shoot?"

She stared out over the lush greenery, following the spiralling path of a hang glider sailing overhead. "There was only Caz and I. We did everything together and he was into extreme sports from an early age. For all his laid-back attitude, he's always been the risk-taker. He dragged me into trouble; I got us out. To look after him I had to be at least as good as he was, sometimes better or he complained I was holding him back."

"Sounds like you pair made a good team," he commented, eyes on the curving road ahead.

"Yes," she replied quietly.

She missed Castor - the twin-bond they'd shared as children sustained both through their turbulent teenage years. The distance Rick put between them had never quite been bridged. Could it ever? So many secrets.

They rode the rest of the short trip in thoughtful silence. As they passed their villa, Alex slowed down.

"Did you want to get changed before meeting up with the others?"

She inspected her clothes. Her t-shirt and shorts weren't exactly glamorous. Brushing at a smudge of dirt on her pants, she screwed up her nose.

"Meh. It's only for an hour or so and I'll be changing into an ugly bridesmaids dress anyway."

"Not all bridesmaids dresses are ugly, you know," he said mildly, pulling up outside Amy's building.

"Seriously?" Kali slid out of the leather seat and made a half-hearted attempt to tie her windblown hair back into some semblance of order. "When was the last time you wore one? And this one's pink!" She waved a hand at herself. "Me, in pink. Ew."

He chuckled, unfolded himself from the car and sauntered around. He tucked a stray strand of hair behind her ear, his hand drifting down to rest on her neck, one thumb caressing the line of her jaw.

"You go have fun and forget everything else. Deal?" He kissed her forehead.

She clenched her teeth and swallowed. "Fun's over. Back to work, I think. This is too good an opportunity to get information. I need to find out his movements if I can; work out when I might be able to...distract him."

He drew in a sharp breath, opened his mouth then shut it again. His hands dropped to his side and his expression shifted back to the remote calm she'd come to recognise as him distancing himself from some painful emotion. What caused it? Spinning away, he gave her a quick, dismissive wave and drove off without a backward glance.

She considered his retreating form for a few seconds then thumbed the buzzer to the villa.

Chapter Twelve

Three and a half hours later, Kali swiped her keycard and shouldered the door to her villa open. Kicking off her shoes, she padded down the hallway and hung the dress-bag she carried up in the cavernous hall closet.

"Hi honey, I'm home!" she called.

"How was work?" Alex's voice drifted out from the bedroom.

She dropped into a squashy couch with a heartfelt sigh. "I'm just not cut out for espionage," she grumbled, "not if it means drinking that much champagne and listening to women tell dirty stories."

"Well, that sounds like fun to me." He appeared in the doorway just as she looked up. "How's the dress?"

Her head spun but that didn't stop her appreciating the sight of him. Hands tucked into the pockets of beautifully tailored dark grey trousers, he leaned against the door frame and gazed down at her with amusement. He wore a longsleeved light grey silk shirt with a Chinese collar and his hair was delectably mussed in a way that made her want to run her fingers through it.

She groaned, leaning her head back on the couch in the hopes that the room would stay still.

"The dress isn't as bad as I thought. Not pink anymore. Max asked her to switch to red. It's a bit flashy for me but s'posed to be a fortunate colour in China. And it now has straps, so at least I don't have to worry about wardrobe malfunctions. Otherwise, it was a complete waste of time." She yawned. "I think Amy intends to spend the whole week drunk if she possibly can. I couldn't get anything useful out of her regarding Max's movements. She had no clue at all, so all we know is the scheduled times he won't be in the room. Sorry."

There was a throaty chuckle overhead. She squinted at him.

"Never mind. I'll try my luck now and you can sleep off the aftereffects of too much champagne." He leaned over and kissed her on the forehead again.

She batted at his face. "Go 'way."

"Your wish is my command." He headed for the door. "I've ordered dinner for you in an hour. There's water on the table in front of you. See you later."

She waved a hand vaguely. The front door clicked shut behind him. She yawned and sank further into the couch, pillowing her head on one of the decorative cushions and stretching out. Much better.

She must have slept, for she woke to a soft knock and a cheery greeting from Jason at the front door. She called him in and sat up with a yawn as he slid the food onto the coffee table in front of the couch.

"Thanks. I don't think we'll need anything else tonight, Jason." She waved him out the door and inspected the food tray without a great deal of enthusiasm. Lifting the silver cover, she laughed aloud. Accompanying a plate of something delicious smelling in chicken, was a packet of painkillers and a packet of fizzy vitamin B tablets. It seemed Alex thought of everything.

She took one of the painkillers and drank the vitamin B, just in case. The rest would go beside the bed in case a headache developed during the night. She rarely drank these days. The aftereffects were too hideous. Today she'd been obliged to drink way more than she intended because of a tendency for the bride and bridesmaids to toast everything and everyone in sight. Tracking the amount in her glass proved impossible with the waiters sloshing champagne into it whenever she so much as blinked for too long.

She ate some of the chicken then put the rest in the fridge and took a shower. Tired and still a little light headed, she came out of the bathroom and eyed the bed. It was only seven thirty. Was that too early to go to bed? Ah, who cared? She was on holidays. There was no TV to watch and her brain was too fuzzy for books or emails. Bed it was.

As she climbed in, naked against the smooth, heavy sheets, she chuckled sleepily. On holiday in a tropical resort and she was going to bed early like some grandmother. Castor would be cross with her.

*****

Swimming out of the depths, head muzzy from sleep and wine, Kali squinted in the darkness. A discreet clock by the bedside read eleven forty five. Still night. Her body lay heavy with the lassitude of deep sleep, so what woke her? There: the sound of someone in her room trying hard to be quiet. She slipped a hand under her pillow. The bed sagged ever so slightly, as someone sat or lay on the memory foam. She lay on her left side, facing the curtained window, blinking in the gloom. A hand touched her right shoulder, lightly - as though testing to see if she was awake.

In a flash, she flipped over, grabbed at the hand and stretched it out, sliding her right hand up its length until she found a neck.

"Don't move," she growled. "I *will* slit your throat."

Muscles tensed under her fingers then a soft chuckle broke the stasis.

"Can I at least switch on a light?" A light flicked on, bathing the room in a soft yellow glow.

"Alex!" She breathed, relief flooding fast after adrenalin ebbed. She let his hand go and withdrew her own. Then she glanced around the room and back at him, reclining on the bed, wearing only boxer shorts and an amused smile. "What are you doing in here? Why are you back so early?"

"They brought in strippers. Not my scene. I left. Nice...er...knife...by the way." He nodded at the wicked blade she still clutched in one hand.

Looking down, she gasped and snatched at the tangled sheets. She was naked. Cheeks flaming, she shoved the knife back under her pillow and rounded on him.

"Strippers? Amy won't be impressed." She tried for blasé but probably came across as confused and embarrassed. "Hang on. What the hell are you doing in here? What about the couch?"

He hitched himself up on one elbow and shrugged his free shoulder, the muscles moving distractingly.

"Hopefully, sleeping." He ran a hand through his disordered hair and yawned. "I'm beat."

"But... but..." Where had she put her clothing? Damn, they were in the dirty clothes pile in the closet. She'd been too tired to ferret around for something to sleep in. She normally slept in the nude, anyway.

He cocked his head to one side, secret humour glimmering. "Did you forget our bet today?"

She blinked in confusion. "But it was whoever won got the bed."

"Yep, and?"

"I wo-" she stopped, tallying the day. "No one won. We tied. So, what? You think that means we should *share* the bed?"

His smile broadened and he patted the crisp white sheets. "Way more comfortable than the couch, believe me."

"Oh no! No way." She edged off the bed, trying to

drag the sheet with her. It was too thoroughly tucked in. Her head spun and she grabbed at the bed to steady herself. It didn't work. How the hell was she supposed to get to the closet?.

He chuckled at her discomfiture. "Kali, relax. I'm not going to leap on you. We can just sleep. I'm tired and it was a long and boring evening."

Curiosity piqued, she hesitated then slid back into bed and stretched out on the extreme edge, ready to run. But did she really want to run? Her whole body thrummed and tingled just from the heat of him. Or sleep? As if she could sleep now. Rolling over onto her side, she propped her head onto one hand and tucked the sheet securely around her breasts.

"No luck then?" Hopefully redirecting the conversation to a less provocative subject would cool her off.

He frowned. "Max is too cagey. He's used to protecting his movements. Very vague about what he was doing the next couple of days." He made a noise of frustration and dropped his head back onto the pillow, studying the ceiling. "It doesn't help that I find it challenging to be in the same room without succumbing to the desire to strangle the little bastard."

That was the most forceful expression he'd used to date. Perhaps Mr Cool wasn't so at the moment. She sighed and mirrored his pose, gazing up at the white, timbered ceiling.

"So I guess it's up to me, then?" she murmured, misliking the sinking sensation in her gut. She shivered at the mental image of Max's hands on her skin. Queasy, she shook herself. No. She could handle him. She could do it. It wouldn't come to anything major anyway - she wouldn't be alone with him long enough for that. So, for Amy, Castor and for Alex she could do it. They were worth it.

"Cold?" Alex shifted, leaning over her and dragging a

blanket up, obviously mistaking the reason for her shiver.

Kali regarded him doubtfully. She'd never sleep if Max kept creeping through her mind and poisoning her thinking. Her treacherous brain had an insidious habit of forecasting the worst possible outcomes if she wasn't careful and didn't replace it with a better visualisation. The problem was: she had the wrong sexual experiences from which to draw. Her history with men lacked…well, a lot of things.

Maybe it was time for a change...

She smiled at herself. What a flimsy rationalisation. It might be the alcohol making her brave but the truth was: she wanted Alex. Had done since the moment they met and she'd fought against it every moment since. What was that old saying? In vino veritas. And so there was.

Was there really anything so wrong about succumbing to their attraction instead?

She reached up and pulled Alex's head down. Would she regret going against every one of her logical reasons for not doing this? Her lips touched his. He tensed, pulling away before she could do anything else. His eyes darkened as he considered her, impassive and cool.

"What was that for?" he asked calmly.

"Me." Her heart thudded so loudly he must be able to hear it. "Because I want..." She closed her eyes for a second and drew a long, slow breath, trying to calm her racing heart and pounding blood.

"Kali," he frowned, "I don't think-"

"Then stop thinking," she cut in. "Stop thinking and do this because I asked you to and because you want to and for no other reason at all." When he still didn't move, she shifted and interlaced her fingers behind his neck. "Please. No strings, no regrets, no agendas, just because we're attracted to each other and we both want to. You are attracted to me, aren't you? Or was that all an act?"

She watched him, heart in her throat. Had she been

fooling herself? Surely her ability to read him wasn't that far off. He was good at wielding his sexuality as a weapon, but he couldn't hide that he found her sexy.

He shook his head slowly, a slow burn lighting in his eyes. "No, not an act. Definitely. But why do you want to?" He leaned in until their lips were just centimetres apart. "It can't help but complicate things between us, no matter how hard we try to keep it cool, you're smart enough to know that."

Her heart pounded again as she gazed openly at him.

"Because...," she stopped. Her cheeks flushed and skin juddered as his hand came to rest on her stomach. "Because I've never felt like this before, I'm afraid of how I feel around you. I don't like being afraid and I want to know..."

"What do you want to know?" He kissed her neck lightly, his breath warm on her skin.

She gasped and clutched at his shoulders, arching her back as the shock tingled through her body.

His lips trailed down to her collarbone and she groaned.

"I know this is going to sound so wrong and I'm sorry."

He lifted his head to look at her and ran a hand delicately over the outline of her leg beneath the sheet, from knee to hip. "Just say it. I won't be offended."

She reached up to trace the line of his brow with her thumb. "I want you because...I can't stop imagining...what's to come with him and I need to know it can be different - I need to have something to hold onto. I've never been with someone who put my needs first and I think you're the sort of person who would. I want to know if I am even capable of feeling...special."

Alex paused, his warm hand still on her body, his face as calm as ever but his eyes were dark and troubled. Then he smiled lopsidedly. "I think we can arrange that. How special do you want to feel?"

"Extremely." She stretched luxuriously. "Like I'm the most important person in the world."

One of his rare, genuine, broad smiles lit his face. "That," he bent and captured her mouth in a searing kiss that left her gasping, "will not be a problem. Trust me." With a crooked, endearing grin he unhooked her fingers and laid her hands palm up on the pillow, "And trust yourself as well."

Kali watched him with a combination of desire and apprehension. He kept eye contact as he trailed his fingers delicately down the soft underside of her arm. She caught her breath at the sight of him: lean, defined, smooth, tanned. He knelt on the bed. She laid a hand wonderingly on his chest. He caught it and kissed the palm before bringing each fingertip to his lips. She held her breath, riding waves of desire that washed through her from breasts to thighs.

Alex placed her hand back on the pillow and shifted closer. "Lie still," he whispered, shaking his head.

"But I...you..." she protested.

He gave her a strait look. "You feeling special, remember? Not me, you."

"I don't think..." She shoved herself half-upright, uncertain and vulnerable.

He lunged toward her, cutting her sentence off by covering her mouth with his. Her arms collapsed and she fell back onto the mattress with a laughing gasp.

He held himself off her, arm muscles shifting with the effort, his expression laughing and frustrated at once.

"Shut up and stop arguing, will you? You think too much. You are worthy of this. Just relax and feel and..." he paused for a moment, amused exasperation segueing into seriousness, "tell me to stop any time if you're not ready. Deal?"

She opened her mouth to argue then nodded. He

flicked a look at her lips and groaned, lowering himself to kiss her again. This time she relaxed and let him lead, exploring his delicious mouth with her tongue, opening hers to his skilled touch. Without breaking the kiss, he shifted his weight to lie beside her. She ran her fingers through his hair, revelling in its thick, silkiness.

Alex peeled her hand free and pressed it back onto the pillow. His fingers drifted down the soft inner side of her arm again, slowing as he trailed closer to her breast. Kali whimpered against his lips, arching her back as fire followed his fingertips and spread through her whole body. Raising his head, he gazed directly into her eyes as he drew the sheet material slowly down. He stopped just short of baring her breast. She groaned, nipples exquisitely sensitised by the scratch of the material. She wanted nothing more than for him to finish what he'd started and just *touch*.

"Oh, please," she murmured, arching her back again.

"Patience," he replied on a chuckle. He trailed a hand down the length of her other outstretched arm and moved that part of the sheet as well. Next he traced along her hairline, twirling one curl through his fingers, gently sweeping his fingertips along her jaw, down her neck and across her décolletage, ever closer to her breasts but never quite close enough.

"Roll onto your stomach," he whispered into her ear, "please."

She opened her mouth to ask why. He gave her a challenging glare and she chuckled. She rolled over, stretching her arms out over her head, wrists crossed, face turned toward Alex's sleek form lying alongside her. He smiled down at her and bent his elbow, resting his cheek on his left hand.

"Do you even know how beautiful you are?" He pulled out the hairtie that held her hair up in its normal messy ponytail, flicking it casually off into the distance.

He ran his fingers through her hair, drawing the black lengths across to expose the nape of her neck. The palm of his hand rested in the middle of her bare back and she sighed, letting her lids drift closed.

"Will you keep your eyes open, Kali?" he murmured. "I'd like to see what you're feeling."

She obliged as he slid his hand lower and drew the sheet softly aside, slipping his hand across her smooth skin in long, languid strokes. One finger slid along the curve of her breast and down the dip and swell of her waist and hip. She shuddered, heat blooming through her, skin goosepimpling in the wake of his touch. His hand swept lower, caressing the mound of her buttocks, tickling the join at the thigh, tantalisingly close but not close enough.

Unable to stand the suspense any longer, she flipped back over and wrapped both hands around his neck.

"If you don't move things along a little faster, I swear I will kick you out and you *can* sleep on the couch." She glared at him and pulled him into a kiss that left her breathless and desperate for more. "Please," she begged.

"You only had to ask." In one swift move he stripped the sheet off her and flung it aside. She gasped and fought against the instinctive urge to cover herself.

He groaned and trailed his fingers down the length of her body. "God you are beautiful. Roll onto your side, that way."

She obligingly rolled onto her right side. Her naked, deliciously-curved body lay, clearly reflected in the full length mirror on the nearby wall. Alex shucked his shorts and lay down behind her, the hard, warm length of his arousal pressing into the small of her back. She shivered, gasping as his hand came to rest on her shoulder. It slid softly, deftly, down the length of her from shoulder to hip and back again, fingers catching in the fine hair at the juncture of her thighs, lingering on the swell and curve of her hip and waist, brushing lightly across her nipple so it sprang to a peak.

By the time he reached her shoulder again, her whole body tingled with anticipation and heat. Watching his hand on her in reflection was voyeuristic; watching him watching her was so hot she almost came when his hand cupped her breast and gently tweaked the nipple.

"Oh..."

Alex shifted slightly, sliding himself between her thighs from behind so gently that, lost in the spikes of pleasure from her nipple, she almost missed his entry into her most secret self. The sensation of being touched and filled, stroked and pleasured overwhelmed her. She closed her eyes, savouring it, prolonging it.

He nipped at her ear. "Keep watching. That is what you look like when you are being well and truly loved. Remember it. Hold onto it. You deserve it."

Kali looked - saw her flushed, starry eyed, breathless expression as his fingers touched her; saw her breast heavy and full in his hand, the nipple cherry with pleasure; saw his broad shoulders and olive-gold skin framing her slight, pale body - and felt secure, treasured, excited beyond belief. She caught his blazing grey eyes in the mirror, saw his heat, his need, his rhythm matching hers. His fingers slid down; stroked her core... and she came apart under his skilled touch.

With a groan and a thrust of his hips, he joined her, his face buried in her neck, fingers still busy pleasuring her; tempting her to come again, with him - which she did, short, sweet and sharp at the feel of him deep inside her.

Chapter Thirteen

She groaned an astonished half-laugh and allowed herself to slide down into heavy-limbed relaxation. Alex pulled her back against his hard chest, brushed aside some strands of hair that fell across her face and kissed her cheek. He slid a lingering hand down the curves of her hip, then up to cup her right breast. His other arm tucked under her neck, his breath sweet and warm on her hair, his body heavy and firm against hers.

"You are…" he sighed, "an extraordinary woman, Kali. Thankyou for trusting me. Go to sleep." He nuzzled her neck. "I'll still be here in the morning, I promise."

This was how it should be. This is what she'd missed out on with Rick. Even this one, fleeting moment of mutual pleasure was more fulfilling than all the planned, choreographed sessions with him. Most of her orgasms had been faked then; he too self-absorbed to care. Now she understood what all the fuss was about - and what she'd been missing all these years.

Damn. She caught the trend of her thoughts. No. This was the definition of a holiday romance, nothing more. Alex remained emotionally unavailable and so, in reality, did she. They both had too many issues to deal with. To make it through this week with her heart intact, she had to remember that.   They both went into this moment eyes open, knowing what she wanted from it. He had obliged, expecting her to want nothing more from him than good memories to take as a shield against the potentially unpleasant ones to come. She needed to remember that, too. This was about Amy, Castor and Alex, not about her.

Once she was certain he slept, she slid free of his embrace and headed for the bathroom. He had used protection, so there was little reason for her to stay there. Wrapping a too-big terry bathrobe around her and flicking off the lamp, she eased the door open and paused, listening to his deep, regular breathing. She slipped out of the bedroom, into the lounge. Stretching out on the couch, she curled her feet under the robe and scrunched a pillow under her head, trying to ignore the hollow ache under her ribs.

It took awhile but eventually she managed to settle and slide into a troubled sleep.

*****

Without blinds, in the main room, Kali woke early. The first rays of sunlight shimmered through glass, reflecting and sparkling off the calm ocean outside. Warmth and light roused her and she sat up with a resigned sigh. The world turned regardless. It was Monday.

She reviewed the day ahead. Nothing much in the morning. Hens night starting at midday for Gods sake. That meant, if she were to get time with Max, it would have to be this morning. She pulled out her phone. It was only five-thirty am. A little early to be calling him to arrange an assignation, especially since he'd've had a late night with the party. Throwing the phone aside, she gazed across at the fishtank, blindly watching their soothing watery meanderings.

What the hell did she do now?

She shoved up off the couch and tiptoed into the bedroom. Snatching clean clothes, bathers, a hat, her book, and a few other random items that might see her through the morning, took only a moment. Alex didn't stir. She stopped by the bed, resisting the urge to slide in next to him and recap last night. No, once was enough. Once was safe. More than that and sex with him would be addictive and a hard habit to break. Sneaking out on silent feet, she closed the door behind her and breathed out.

Now to stay out of his way until lunchtime.

At about eight Alex sent a text with nothing more than the word 'ok?'. She stared at it for a long time before replying with an equally brief 'yes' and turning it off. What else could she say, really? Especially when she didn't know the answer.

The morning passed swiftly enough. She swam in the ocean, showered in the public changerooms and breakfasted at the cafe, all the time firmly redirecting her thoughts whenever they wandered toward contemplating Alex's hands, his mouth, his body, the awe in his eyes as he touched her. Dammit.

At ten she judged Max should have recovered enough and sent him a text saying she was free. She got a polite reply saying he regretted that he was obliged to fly to the mainland and would return Tuesday evening for the ball. He looked forward to catching up with her on Wednesday perhaps.

Sighing, she dropped the phone back into her beach bag and leaned back in the deck chair she currently occupied. What now? It would have been better to get it over and done with. That would solve all her problems - get rid of Max and she was rid of the temptation that was Alex as well. Now why did that cause a twinge of pain in her chest?

She tipped her hat down over her nose to block out the sun. This was all way too complicated.

At eleven fifteen an alarm went off on her phone, reminding her she had to change for the Hens party starting at midday. Now for the dangerous moment. She'd been a coward to slip out without talking to Alex but she had no experience in these things. It was safer to pretend nothing much important had happened. Hopefully he would see it the same way and act accordingly.

With a thudding heart, she swiped the keycard and pushed open the door to the villa.

"Alex?" Her voice sounded high and timorous. She grimaced at her reflection in the hall mirror. Get a grip, Kali. You're a tough single woman of the twenty first century.

"Here." He hailed her from the kitchen, sounding perfectly normal.

With a deep breath to steel herself, she pasted on a smile and padded up the hall.

He was rummaging in the fridge with his back to her, so she took a moment to admire his lean, incredible physique again. Her body thrummed to life, just looking at him. She stifled a groan. He'd obviously been swimming as his hair was wet and mussed. His beautiful, dark-olive skin still glistened and his swim shorts were damp. He glanced back over his shoulder, eyebrows uplifted coolly, expression calm and unfazed as usual.

"Lunch?" He waved a hand at the ingredients spread over the bench. "I had them send over the makings. I'm a bit over cafe lunches."

"Uh, no. Thanks." She hesitated, slightly nonplussed by his offhand acceptance of her vanishing act. "I have to shower and change. I think the Hens night starts with a lunch."

He said nothing, apparently dismissing her as he concentrated on making a sandwich.

Mildly annoyed, she headed for the bedroom.

"Oh," she added, halfway through the door, "I texted Max and apparently he's gone to the mainland and won't be back until Tuesday evening. So I couldn't see him today. I'm sorry."

Alex paused, his hands still. Just for a moment, Kali

got the impression that he held some vast pool of internal tension, perhaps anger, in ruthless check; that his calm was superficial and the result of tight self-control.

"And you would have?" He studied her coolly, apparently composed and relaxed.

She blinked, taken aback. "Of course! How could you doubt it? I'd do anything for Amy and stopping her from marrying a complete bastard is the best thing I could ever do - even if she hates me."

"Yes," he nodded, returning to his sandwich, "of course. Well," he gave her a quick smile that didn't reach past his mouth, "have a fun afternoon. If you come in late just head for the bed. I'll sleep out here." He picked up his sandwich and strode out to the verandah.

She stared after him, bemused and hurt. What the hell was that all about? Surely last night had been mutually agreeable and he couldn't be angry with her about that, could he?

Retreating, she showered fast and grabbed an outfit from the closet; a white, floaty cocktail dress with green straps and a delicate green fern print over one leg. She dressed without really seeing herself in the mirror. Slapping on makeup and tidying her hair, she slipped into a pretty pair of green, high-heeled sandals and emerged from the bedroom. Maybe he'd be in a better mood now.

No such luck. Alex sat on the couch with his feet up on the coffee table, apparently absorbed in a self-help success book. He raised his head when she appeared and, just for a moment, his expression softened to appreciation. Then it closed up into distance. He marked his page, set the book down and stood, with a jerk of his chin toward the phone.

"Call Jason when you're ready to come back. It's not a big island but you won't be able to walk far in those shoes." He laid his hands on her shoulders, fingers biting into her upper arms, his eyes flat and hard in spite of the faint curve to his mouth.

"Alex, I'm sorry..." she began, not really knowing what to apologise for.

He shook his head. "No need. You've done nothing wrong. It's all fine, Kali. As long as you're ok, we're good. Now go," he smiled again, more genuinely, "before I say or do something I'll regret." With that, he spun on his heel and walked out the glass doors, striding purposefully toward the beach until he disappeared from view in the glare and salt.

What the hell was with him? Surely it was meant to be women who got all bent out of shape over a one night stand? What would he regret saying or doing?

Oh. She pressed a hand to her stomach against the flowering of sick disappointment. Of course. She represented his only chance of getting information from Max. He was afraid he'd blown it by sleeping with her. It meant nothing to him and he was afraid she'd get all twisty about it, back out and leave him unable to complete his five year revenge plan. That explained his question about going through with it.

She sighed. Men.

Eschewing Jason's driving services, she walked over to the restaurant where the girls were meeting. Once there, she tried her hardest to be caught up in the experience, for Amy's sake. Of course it was fun - the twenty or so women were a fun bunch; an interesting mix from all areas of Amy's life: two minor Hollywood celebrities; Amy's friends from around the world as well as her mother and a couple of extended family members. Amy excelled great at keeping in touch with her girlfriends and was universally liked. The group were intelligent, hilarious and the afternoon passed quickly up to the point where they began to make little sense and the champagne took over where brains left off.

Kali was one of the few to watch what she drank.

Something in her just wouldn't quite let her get into the free for all drinking frenzy that possessed the others. By six o'clock, things were fairly out of hand. Amy had hired a top of the line band and the women were having a blast dancing and spilling drinks. By eight o'clock, when the male strippers appeared, Kali reached her limit. She slipped away, leaving a screaming, giggling mob of unruly women well behind.

After a cool walk on the beach, sandals in hand, she reluctantly made her way back to the cabin. It was dark. Had Alex gone to bed already? Was he expecting her to join him? Or had he left the bed for her? Damn. There was no way of telling from outside, where he slept.

He was right: sleeping with him had complicated things. She'd been stupid and selfish to think it would be otherwise.

Letting herself in through the main entrance, she flicked on a small desklamp. The main room was empty and clean. A folded piece of paper lay on the bench.

Gone to the mainland. Back tomorrow evening. The bed's all yours.

Alex.

Dumbfounded and bereft, she sank onto a couch and read the note again. Was he *that* angry with her? Surely not. Surely sneaking out this morning wasn't that unforgivable.

Common sense crowded in as she read it a third time. No, if he'd gone to the mainland and was coming back Tuesday night it must be something to do with Max. Everything he did was filtered through that paradigm. He'd followed his target, in case he got a chance he didn't have here. It made sense, of course, but it didn't stop her from feeling like crap.

Alone, miserable, and angry with herself for letting his absence affect her, she undressed and curled up in the big bed, trying not to smell his spicy masculine scent on the

pillow under her head.
*****

Tuesday dawned sullen and grey and Kali woke late. Inspecting the stormy skies she tasted relief in the promise of rain. The tennis and golf matches Amy had planned for today wouldn't go ahead in this weather and there was no chance of running into Max. Amy wouldn't surface until at least three, based on her alcohol intake of the previous evening. So chances were there would be nothing organised to do all day until the costume party that evening. Even the prospect of scuba diving or parasailing dulled when faced with no like-minded companion and a stormy day.

After showering and changing, she padded restlessly around the villa. Raindrops thundered against the glass and splashed up off the timber decking so heavily that the beach, just ten metres away, was invisible in a wall of grey. So much for the tropical idyll. So far there'd been more rain than sunshine.

She ate late enough to call it lunch, rather than breakfast, barely even tasting the food. Then, stir-crazy, she headed for the door, only to be driven back inside by a windy squall that dumped a deluge on the shivering tropical plants outside and soaked her from the knees down.

Returning to the lounge she yanked out a book at random from the shelf and tried to read it. Bored after ten pages, she tried another. Still no good.

Flipping open her laptop, she passed a couple of hours catching up on emails, responding to quote requests and answering phone messages. It did nothing to soothe her restlessness but at least she'd accomplished something. Shutting it at long last, she checked the clock. Three thirty pm.

She picked up her phone, debating whether to call Amy for that much-delayed catchup. Something in her rebelled. She just couldn't sit around talking inconsequentialities with the burden of expectation weighing on her mind. And there was always the chance Amy would notice her nervousness and call her on it. They knew each other too well.

She just wanted to get this meeting with Max over with. It preyed on her mind and twisted her stomach into knots. Wednesday was too far away.

Staring at her phone, she debated with herself. Finally, fingers shaking, she texted Max, querying when he'd be back, asking if they could get together before the costume ball started at eight, rather than waiting until Wednesday. After a fifteen minute, tension-filled wait, he sent back an affirmative. He would come straight from the airport, drop his laptop in his suite and would then meet her at a cafe near the marina at five.

That sounded safe enough. And perfect.

She sent a query off to Alex. Would he be back in time? Had she given Max too much notice? He, too, took several long minutes to respond. He would be back at four thirty and would be ready. Nothing else. No good luck; no thankyou. So cold and clinical.

Her heart thumped uncomfortably and her palms sweated as she contemplated the meeting. Now time sped. Every time she looked at the clock another half hour zipped past, leaving her closer to the moment of truth.

At halfpast four she went into the closet and picked out what to wear. Not wanting to carry a purse, she chose long, loose cargo shorts and slipped her wallet into the back pocket. A small knife went into an ankle sheath under her high-topped runners - a thigh sheath would be a bit obvious if his hands went where she thought they might. She shivered as she slipped on a loose green tshirt.

Tying her hair into a practical ponytail she secured a few stray ends with bobbypins and stood before the mirror and grimaced. She hadn't exactly dressed for seduction.

Her costume for the ball, a stunning designer creation

based on an eighteenth century dress, had been delivered and hung in the closet. She ran a hand over the green silk confection and sighed. If things went to plan she'd never wear it now.

She dropped her phone into a pocket and headed for the door, amazed at her utter calm and detachment. If she shut out the next hour and avoided thinking about it, she could make herself move. Shutting it out was a good thing. This was not something she wanted to dwell on lest she panic and back out. After all, there was every likelihood that nothing major would happen and it would all be over in half an hour.

A quick text to Alex to say she was going to the Marina elicited no response. That worried her for a moment but, if he was in the middle of landing, he may not be able to answer. Both annoyed and relieved, she called for Jason.

The storm had swept out to sea and the sun sparkled through dripping leaves as she stood outside, waiting. When Jason picked her up, she managed to work in, amongst his cheerful conversation, a request to go and collect Amy at no later than five fifteen and bring her to the marina.

That was the only really tricky bit of the plan. If Amy should query Jason, the whole thing might come undone. A combination of a hangover and trust ought to do the trick, ensuring she would just come without question.

Her stomach sank. She ran sticky hands across her shorts. How had things come to this, and so fast? Well, at least it was somewhere public, so things couldn't get too out of hand.

Would Alex and Lacey be able to get into position? Would Max have arranged for his laptop to be guarded? Would they be able to ghost it? Would Amy be out of the way? There were just so many damned variables it made her teeth ache with stress and frustration.

That distracted, worried fear carried her through to the moment where she stood outside the café. Then the weight of what she intended crashed in and she almost bolted. No. Hand on the cool aluminium doorhandle to the cafe she drew a long breath and squared her shoulders. She could do this. For Alex, Amy and Castor. One small sacrifice to make three people happy. It was worth it and she would survive. She'd survived worse.

She pushed the door open. He rose to meet her.

"Max." She accepted his hug, even holding it a little longer than convention dictated.

He looked her up and down as they sank into the seats. This cafe was, if possible, even more up-market than the one at the shooting range. It was all glass, marble and steel, shining and cool in the glittering afternoon sun. The first hints of a spectacular sunset sparkled off the water, dimmed by light-sensitive tinted windows overlooking the small harbour. A row of seagulls perched, neatly lined up, on a railing outside the window. It was expensively picturesque.

A waitress came, poured iced, expensive water, and asked if they wanted to order. Max waved the girl away as Kali refused. She felt too sick in the stomach to eat anything.

"You're looking well," he said, meticulously polite. "How did the hens night go?"

She sipped at her water. "Parties aren't really my thing so I left a bit early. It was fun, though. Amy had a great time." Her mouth was dry, her palms sweating. She drank again, covering nervousness.

"Yes, so I understand. She didn't call me until after one." His tone was cool, as though he spoke of a mere acquaintance. "Now I know you don't have much time before you have to start getting ready for the ball, so how about we get right to it?"

Did he mean the double-entendre built into that

sentence? Possibly, possibly not.

"Sure."   She tried to ignore the fluttering in her stomach. "What's this proposal of yours?"

"Well," Max signalled the maitre de over and handed him a fifty dollar bill, "I have all the details on my yacht." He nodded out the window at the collection of white masts and sleek lines bobbing outside. "Let's adjourn there and we'll be back in time to get you dressed and ready, I promise."

She hesitated. She'd instructed Jason to bring Amy to the marina café and tell her Max had sent for her. If she didn't find him, Amy was smart enough to ask and undoubtedly the maitre de would tell her where they'd gone.

"Sure, I'll just duck to the Ladies first." She bolted to the bathroom and texted Alex the change of plans.

He didn't reply. She talked at her reflection in the gilt-framed mirror over the sink, willing herself to be calm and level-headed. After all, it was just a couple of kisses.

Heart racing she rejoined Max, revolted by his touch on her elbow as he guided her out of the cafe and down the gently swaying marina pier toward his boat. The sticky afternoon air felt heavy in her lungs after the airconditioning; harder to breathe. Or maybe that was just because way her heart thumped against her ribs.

Chapter Fourteen

"Wow." Kali breathed a genuine grunt of surprise, when they reached the berth. "She's a beauty."

"Yes." Max admired the lines of his boat with her. "She is. Shall we step aboard? Watch the swell." He handed her up to a crewman who took her hand and helped her over the gunwale. "She's just my island hopper I keep here. The yacht we'll travel back to Malaysia in is, of course, too big to moor here. Amy and I will meet her in deeper waters up the coast and transfer for our honeymoon."

It was a beautiful vessel. At least sixty feet and built for sailing speed as well as luxury. Its white sides were blinding in the afternoon sun. Expensive brass and timber finishes gleamed in softly polished, curved perfection.

Following Max, Kali swayed down the port side and cast one last look at land. A golf cart pulled up at the end of the pier. She caught a glimpse of Amy's distinctive blonde hair and scarlet lipstick. Damn. Showtime.

In the main area under the deck, she had little time to admire the fixtures and silk-cushioned decor. She had to buy Alex some time. Amy was here a little early and Max hadn't yet made a move. So far there was no reason for Amy to break up with him. She'd have to play the vamp and move things along so Amy had a scene to judge when she arrived in a couple of minutes.

"So." She faced Max, only to find him well within her personal space already, his eyes gleaming with dark, secret knowledge. "Um, what did you want to see me about?" Her voice sounded childishly breathless and cracked. She cleared her throat.

"I think you know, Kalisa," he murmured, stepping even closer.

His hands slid up her arms and gripped with surprising strength, pushing her backward until she hit the timber wall with a force that knocked the breath from her lungs. While her instincts screamed at her to fight back, to incapacitate him, to get away as fast as she could; logic stood its ground and told her to play along. She needed to buy Alex time, and wait for Amy. So she let him kiss her, shutting her mind to his too-soft lips on hers; his fingers bruising her arms, his thigh pushing between her knees.

"Max!" She gasped as he slid his hands under her shirt and grabbed at her breasts with painful roughness. "What about Amy? We shouldn't-"

"Forget her for a moment, Kalisa." He frowned at her, eyes hooded and glittering. "You know I've wanted you since the moment I first met you. I might be marrying Amy but it's you I want in my bed right now." He stripped her shirt off over her head and threw it aside, staring at her in such a way that she felt filthy and longed to end it now - painfully for him.

Footsteps sounded outside. Kali grabbed at his shoulders and pulled him back into a kiss, dropping her hands and letting his do the work as the door opened beside them.

"Max! Kali!" Amy's incredulous cry split the two apart.

Kali stepped aside, both relieved and guiltily embarrassed. She snatched up her shirt and dragged it on. The horror on Amy's face was almost unbearable. She wanted to reassure her; to explain. She couldn't. Alex needed a little more time. They'd agreed on half an hour and it'd only been twenty minutes. He hadn't called, so that meant the job wasn't done. Somehow she had to string out this disgusting little scene a little longer.

"Amy," she tried, "it's not what you think."

Amy scowled at her, folding her arms across her chest. "Really."

"No, indeed." Max's smooth, amused tone interrupted their burgeoning catfight.

Both women turned to him in surprise. He didn't sound like a guilty fiancé sprung in the act of cheating. Kali caught sight of his hand and gasped. Amy's hands flew to her mouth.

"What on earth? Max, have you gone insane?" Amy took an angry half-step toward him but stopped, paling when he swung the gun he held toward her.

"No, I'm not insane at all." He smiled coldly at them. "I'm actually quite pleased with how this has all come together. I assume Kalisa is responsible for getting you here and in that she's saved me some effort. Although," his gaze measured Kali's body, "I would have preferred a few more minutes alone with her. Excuse me a moment." Keeping a careful watch on both women, he flipped out his phone, dialled and spoke into it in Mandarin.

"Is he secure? No? What do you mean?" His nostrils flared, jaw clenching as he spat a curse. "Incompetent. Secure his plane. He is not to leave the island. Get the yacht ready and cast off. Now. We depart in ten minutes."

Kali kept her face still, her heart lifting. He obviously didn't know she understood.

Hope hammered her heart and flushed into her cheeks. Alex was alive and free; so far.

"Max!" Amy's voice was shrill. "What the hell is going on? What's happening? Why do you-"

"Oh, do shut up. I've had enough of your narcissism and whining." Max directed a cold glare on her and Amy shut her mouth, her expression bewildered. "Thankyou," he continued. "Now both of you will walk quite calmly over to that couch and sit down. Kalisa, Amy will walk between us and I will have the gun to her chest every step of the way. Should you even attempt to attack me, run or escape, I promise I will have no hesitation in shooting her. Do you understand?"

Kali nodded, her heart racing against her ribs, mouth dry, hands slippery with sweat. Various options for taking the gun from him shuttled across her mind, only to be dismissed. He stayed carefully out of her reach. He knew what he was doing and he knew what she was capable of. He wasn't taking any risks.

Where was Alex?

The brilliant, tropical afternoon made the whole thing ridiculous. Calm and serene, luxurious yachts bobbed at anchor just outside; people on the one next door engrossed in their conversation and drinks. They were barely fifty metres away. Would they hear a gunshot? Would they hear a scream? Surely a kidnapping wasn't happening right under their noses. Things like that didn't happen. Any minute now *someone* would notice what was happening behind the wide glass windows; see the gun and ask what was going on. Surely. Someone.

Where the hell was Alex?

Kali kept hoping, right up until the point where the anchor chain clanked into action; right up to the point where the big engines thrummed to life; right up to where and she and Amy were thrust into a tiny crew cabin with two bunkbeds and a cramped head. As she stepped into the room, Kali turned back. Max raised the gun. She kept her hands in sight.

"What are you going to do with us?" She tried to steady her voice.

He gave her a knowing, smug little inclination of his head. "First you'll be bait to bring Alex to heel, then, when

I've dealt with him, you'll be handed over to some...friends of mine who have a taste for western women. Sold, you might say. For more than a mere three hundred thousand, too. How I enjoyed forcing the bidding up and making Alex pay so much." He gestured for her to turn around. Reluctantly, she did.

The last thing she saw was Amy's shocked expression, then pain exploded in her head and blackness enfolded her.

*****

A sudden lurch jolted her to full wakefulness. With consciousness, came pain. Her head throbbed rhythmically. It ached through her whole body. She opened her eyes slowly. A bright lightbulb overhead blinded her and she turned her head to escape it. That brought on a surge of nausea and she groaned. She lay on a rough-carpeted floor in a room that swayed and moved unpleasantly.

"Oh, thank God you're ok." Amy's tear-ravaged, worried face swam into view.

Kali sucked a long, deep breath, willing the pain in her head to go. It didn't work.

"For a given value of ok, I guess," she croaked. Her mouth filled with saliva as the boat lurched again and nausea returned in full force. "Hang on."

Clambering unsteadily to her feet, she edged around Amy and made her way to the head, clutching at the door frame. There she was noisily sick, ignoring Amy's faint protest. Marginally better, she washed her face and rinsed out her mouth at the tiny sink. There was no mirror. Probably a good thing, really.

Her skull throbbed in time with the thrum of boat engines. Gingerly she fingered the lump on the back of her head where Max had hit her with the gun-butt. That had been totally uncalled for. Then again, if she kidnapped someone with martial arts training, she'd take them out of commission as well.

She swayed back out into the tiny cabin and sat down on the bottom bunk, hands tucked under her thighs, head down, unable to believe how horribly wrong things had gone. Was there a point at which she could've taken control and fixed it? All her training at the dojo told her the time to foil a kidnapping lay right at the beginning but she couldn't have risked Amy's life to save her own, could she?

She squinted up. Amy sat on the floor, her back against the wall, elbows on knees, hands hiding her face, silent and still. There was nothing Kali could say to explain or comfort her at the moment. She had no hope herself.

"How long was I out?" She checked her watch but it was missing. Her phone was gone too, along with her wallet. Obviously Max's men had searched her while she lay unconscious. She shuddered in distaste. What else had they touched? Wait! The knife strapped to her ankle. Pulling down the sock, she found the sheath - empty.

Despair washed over her with such force that she dropped her head into her hands and groaned. The pounding in her skull drowned out all logical thought. There was *something* she had to remember. What was it? She leaned forward, pressing her palms against her aching head. Scalding tears seeped out from under her eyelids, unbidden.

The thin mattress sank a little and Amy's arm draped around her shoulders. "About an hour, I think," she murmured, resting her head gently against Kali's. "Bad?"

"The worst. Did Max come back and say anything?"

Amy shuddered. "No, he just sent his men in to search us. What's going on? Why do I get the idea that there's something you're not telling me? What was that scene I walked in on? You never really liked Max." A hint of remembered jealousy coloured her tone.

Kali sighed. "It's a long story."

"We have time, I'd say," came the acerbic reply. "Astonish me."

"Basically, Alex has a history with Max neither of us knew about when he bid for me on Ebay."

"What sort of history?" Amy glared, taking her arm from around Kali's shoulders and folding it with the other, across her chest.

Kali sent her friend a weary look. "My head is killing me. If you'll just be quiet I promise I'll tell you everything. Deal?"

She opened her mouth, shut it again, screwed up her nose, then nodded.

So Kali related what she knew of Alex, his sister and her husband and Max's involvement in the story. She hesitated over Castor's part in it, then decided she had to tell it, if only to lend credibility to Alex. By the time she finished, Amy stared in open-mouthed astonishment, apparently unable to speak for the first time Kali had ever seen.

"Oh my God," Amy whispered at last. "I've just remembered." She opened wide blue eyes at Kali. "It was Max. Max made a joke that I should put you on Ebay as an option for getting you to the island. It was Max that changed his schedule so that his plane wasn't available to collect you. Do you think he planned the whole thing? But how could he? You said Alex changed his name so Max wouldn't connect him up with his sister." She nibbled on a fingernail, regarding the floor intently. She dropped her hand and sat up straight. "Oh!"

Kali squinted up at her, her brain still too thick and painful to think it through.

"Her purse," Amy said, clutching at Kali's arm.

"What about it?"

"Most people," Amy said, anger creeping into her voice, "women especially, carry photos of family on their phone or in their purse. Of course Alex's sister would, too.

How could Alex and Castor have missed that?"

Kali pressed a thumb to her temple. She was right. Had to be. Hell, Shelley's wedding photos were probably on her phone, with Alex in the bridal party; and Castor, too. This whole time, all these years Alex thought he'd stalked Max unrecognised and unseen - Max must have known. At least for some of the time. Maybe not right at the start.

She sat up straight. "Ames, how did you meet Max again?"

Amy's scarlet nails dug into Kali's arm again. "No! Surely not. No one could be that devious! I met him at an after party for the Logies in Sydney."

"Has he ever, after that, shown any interest whatsoever in hanging around at Hollywood type parties?"

Her shoulders slumped. "No. Once he even said he hated them. He admitted he'd gone to that party specifically to meet me. I was flattered! But it was all...he just...he wanted to get to Caz and through him to Alex." She sniffed, tears sliding down her cheeks. "But why didn't he just go after you?" she said at last. "Why this whole charade of pretending...to...want to marry me?"

Kali shrugged impatiently. "I don't know. I keep a pretty low profile. Maybe you were easier to find and easier to target. Maybe he didn't know about me, only about Alex and Caz. You do have a photo of you and Caz on your Facebook page; and Alex probably had private emails between himself and his sister on her phone. Max might've even had people hack his email account and connect him to Caz and through Caz to you. Who knows, Ames? The point is he found the connections between us and used them. Now we just need to work out how to get the hell out of here." Kali wrapped her in a hug and held on.

They sat in silence for awhile until Amy stiffened again.

"Caz!" she breathed, shoving Kali's hands aside.

"He'll go after him as well. He was really upset when Caz said he wasn't coming to the wedding. I thought he wanted to make the day perfect for me but he was just trying to get everyone in one place. Kali," she gripped Kali's hands, showing real alarm for the first time, "we have to get out of here and warn Caz."

She nodded, regretting the movement as it sent shooting pains through her skull. "First things first. Did you happen to hear a plane go overhead when we left dock?"

"The engines are too loud. Why? Oh, Alex. Do you think he'll know where we are?"

"I'm not going to hold my breath," Kali muttered. "Max told his men to close the airport and catch him. Even if he did fly out, he won't know which way the boat's going and I saw at least four other yachts about the same size leaving the harbour. Alex'll probably head toward international waters but Max told me his ocean-going yacht is moored further up the coast in a deep-water harbour. We can't wait to be rescued, Ames. We have no idea where we're going and the further we go the more chance there is of being taken out of Australian waters."

"But even if we get off the boat, it must be close to full night," Amy protested, "how would we know where to go?"

Kali groaned, holding her head. "I don't know yet. Let me think."

She climbed onto the top bunk and peered out the small porthole. A series of lights twinkled in the distance. Too close-set and high to be boats, they glimmered against a darkness that blotted out the last vestiges of sunset. Land. It must be. Swimming to it wasn't her idea of a good time but it gave them at least a chance of survival. Assuming she could get them off this tub. It might be just an island, or it could be the mainland. Which one didn't matter, the light-speckled darkness seemed to be only a kilometre or so away. That was their best chance.

The question was: could they swim that far when she was clearly concussed and Amy had never exactly listed swimming on her cv?

Shoving that aside for later, she pushed her aching brain to consider the next questions - how to get out of this room and how to get past the guards and crew that must be on the boat? Even if there were only Max, his two guards and maybe two or three crew, it was still highly unlikely she and Amy could sneak past unnoticed.

Resolutely, she shelved that as well. She'd cross that bridge when they came to it. First things first: getting out of this room.

"Amy, I don't suppose you have any handy lockpicks on you do you?" Bobbypins really weren't strong enough to pick doorlocks with.

"All I have is my clothes." Amy plucked at her blouse.

"Clothes..." Kali tried to force her mind to think logically. "Underwire!"

Jerking up her shirt, she twisted and plucked at her bra until she managed to poke the underwire out through the fabric. Pulling the first free, she then worked on the second. Amy watched in bewilderment.

"OK," Kali took a deep breath. "Now we need to get ready. Once we're out, we'll have to be quick and quiet. By the slope of the wall, I'd say we're up toward the bow." She pointed toward the curving wall behind the beds. "I think most boats have the sleeping quarters up the bow end and the eating and dining and open air areas toward the back. If we go sternward, there's a bigger chance of meeting the crew at this time of night. If we for to the bow, we might just be able to sneak out the forward hatch. It will mean a long drop into the water though, and a risk of being seen by the pilot. Let's get some things ready to take with us."

"How do you know so much about boats?" Amy

grumbled. "You could have asked me. I might have been on this one for all you know."

Kali looked at her wearily. "Have you?"

"Well, no, but neither have you." She folded her arms mulishly.

"Rick rented one almost the same when he was…trying to impress me. Ames, can we not argue about who's right just at this particular moment? When we're on dry land you can get as mad at me as you like for getting you into this, I promise. But right now, I'd like to get us both out alive."

Chapter Fifteen

Kali listed what she wanted and Amy nodded, her expression apprehensive again. Together they ripped two sheets lengthways and knotted them into a rope. Next they both drank as much water as they could hold and kicked off their shoes. Kali rummaged under the lowest bunk and pulled out two life-jackets. First she found and ripped out the gps tracker stitched into them. Then she tugged off her shorts and shirt and tied them to the jacket. Amy followed her lead.

"Right. You carry the jackets and the rope, Amy. I'm going to take point and I'll need my hands free if we meet anyone," Kali said grimly. Amy's eyes widened but she nodded. Her hands trembled as she took the jackets.

Kali picked up the underwire pieces. She crouched in front of the door and went to work on the lock. All the time, she listened intently for footsteps outside the door. Only her own harsh breathing, the slap of water on the hull and the occasional scuff as Amy shifted restlessly behind her broke the diesel-fumed silence. Since speed was the issue, and the lock simple, she inserted one as a torsion wrench and raked the pins with the other. It took several tries but the pins slipped away, one by one, until the lock moved freely.

She straightened, worked the wire back into her bra, and twisted the handle slowly and carefully. Opening the door a crack, she peered out in to the dim-lit corridor. Empty. A little further and she was able to ease one eye past the frame and check again. Still empty.

With a nod to Amy, she opened the door fully and slipped, on silent, careful feet, into the short, narrow corridor. Amy followed. They paced toward the bow of the ship, checking behind for crew. They passed two closed doors, both of which blessedly remained that way. At the end of the corridor, a final door faced them. Judging from the space left to traverse, it must lead to the master bedroom. Kali gripped the handle, praying it would be empty. There wasn't anywhere else to go, after all.

It was.

A quick inspection of the gasp-worthy timber-and-gilt decoration and the massive, silk-sheeted bed that dominated the room, showed little of use to them in escaping. The sight of a half-open safe and its contents made her groan but Kali dismissed Amy's whispered question. There was nothing she could do right now and no point in getting into a lengthy discussion about it, either.

Instead, she focussed on the forward hatch, directly above her head. She locked the door behind them and dragged a chair under the hatch. It wasn't going to be high enough. A wooden chest placed under the chair made a serviceable, if a bit unsteady, ladder. The sway and toss of the boat would make it tricky but with a little luck they'd be able to climb out.

No such luck - the hatch was bolted from the outside.

She dropped down to the floor and hurriedly put the chair and chest back where they'd come from. There must be another way out. She closed her eyes, thinking through the miasma of pain behind them. Yes, of course.

There, tucked into a corner of the room was a small

door that ought to give access to the anchor chain room. .

And they were in luck. The tiny, dark room smelled of saltwater, fish and rust. Once Kali spotted the hatch overhead and found it unlocked, she gestured to Amy, who ducked out to unlock Max's room door, then closed the service door softly behind them. This was better, anyway. If they left a chair and chest stacked up in Max's locked room, the whole game would be up. Vanishing without evidence might buy a few more hours.

Kali cautiously poked her head out and inspected the rocking deck surface for feet. There, facing away from her, on the port side. Someone with expensive shoes stood at the railing, smoking a cigarette by the orange glow haloing his head.

Expecting an outcry at any second, she eased her body out onto the cold deck and rolled clear. High above, in his insulated, glassed cabin, a crewmember piloted the boat. His back was toward her, his head tilted as he threw down a glass of some brown liquid; hopefully alcohol that would make his vision blurry. He moved away from the window and she let out the breath she'd held.

She crept up behind the crewman on deck. Snaking one arm around his neck from behind, she collapsed his knees with a well-aimed kick. His cigarette landed on the deck and rolled off into the dark water, vanishing. He grunted, scrabbling at her arm with blunt fingers, reaching over his head to grab at hers. She ducked lower. With his thick neck locked in the crook of her elbow, she dragged him onto his back and kept the sleeper hold on until he went limp. Then she released him, feeling for a pulse. Still alive. That hold would kill if she held it a few seconds too long.

Scanning the deck, she hauled him to the hatch and rapped him sharply on the head with his own gun butt. That should keep him under til morning. As an afterthought, she unstrapped his waterproof watch and placed it around her own arm. It was loose but should stay on. The luminous dial read just after six-thirty pm. The gun she tucked into the waistband of her underwear.

By the time she got back to the hatch, Amy had pushed both life jackets and the rope out and pulled herself painfully up onto the deck. Kali gave her a hand. Together they bound and gagged the sailor with scraps from one of the sheet lengths and lowered him into the anchor room. Hopefully that would buy them some time. Knotting the remaining sheet low around a railing post, she put the life jacket around her neck. Quickly and quietly, she lowered Amy, and then herself, into the ocean.

The chill, black water made her gasp. The curling white wake slapped her face. Saltwater got up her nose and into her mouth. It stung the back of her head and the vile taste made her gag. She coughed and sputtered, blinking and rubbing her eyes as the yacht sped by. It was under power and moving against a slight breeze in a calm sea. It should be well away in a short time.

When its red and blue running lights and thrumming motor noise faded satisfactorily into the darkness, she called out for Amy and they found each other. Clinging together in the cold, dark vastness of the say, they laughed and cried in relief and release from immediate fear.

Then Kali, pragmatic, sobered and searched for light-beacons. There. Shimmering in the darkness; tiny, twinkling will-o-the-wisps of hope. They tied the life vests to their ankles and struck out smoothly towards the distant lights of shore. As she swam, the gun slipped free and sank into the black below. Kali swore.

*****

Before long, Kali regretted their method of escape. After what felt like an hour, but was really only half that, she and Amy clung to each other and their life vests for a short spell. Trembling with cold and exhaustion, they stared at the promise of survival. The lights on shore seemed no closer than half an hour ago. It didn't *feel* like they swam against a current. She must have underestimated the distance. Either that or the head knock was worse than she thought.

"I don't know if I can do this." Amy sobbed, spitting saltwater and shivering.

Kali pulled herself together. She had to get them to safety. It was her job and hers alone. There was no time or space to feel sorry for herself. Amy needed her to be strong. She put an arm around Amy and held her, letting her relax and stop swimming for awhile.

"Tell you what, you put the life jacket on and I'll tow you for awhile. We'll get there, Ames. Have I ever let you down yet?" Kali forced her tone to be lighthearted. Inside she squashed a moment of self-doubt.

Wrapping an arm around Amy, she settled into a slow sidestroke through the cold, smooth water. Luckily the waves were just a small swell, the evening calm and clear. Stars glittered above and below. Bioluminescence swirled into greenish vortexes beneath each stroke of her hand. Under other circumstances it would be beautiful.

Every once in a while she checked forward to judge direction and backward to check for the boat. Even though they'd done their best to disguise their disappearance, their absence could still be discovered before morning. If that happened, the boat would return to find them floating helplessly in the sea.

*****

Looking shoreward again, sometime later, she almost cried out in relief. The lights *were* closer this time. Much closer. She tried, vainly, to judge the distance.

"It shouldn't be more than about half an hour, Ames." She panted, spitting saltwater out of her mouth and blowing it out of her nose. She'd swallowed more than she wanted to and it sat unpleasantly in her stomach, adding to the nausea generated by the ache in her head.

She couldn't feel either fingers or toes. The icy water sapped strength and brainpower. Her foot cramped and she paused to stretch it out. The sharp pain drew a whimper, quickly suppressed, from her. Amy shifted, wriggled free and rolled over to swim beside her instead.

Her blue eyes were dark holes in the faint starlight. "I'm sorry. I'm so sorry I've been such an idiot and got us into this."

Kali managed a laugh, swimming more easily now without the load. "Believe me, you don't have any reason to apologise. There was no way you could've known what Max...was doing. Just keep swimming Amy. When we get to shore we'll find a motel with a hot bath and we'll sleep for a week." Exhausted, she put her life jacket on and paddled slowly towards the lights; desperate for the warmth and safety of shore.

An eternity later the water warmed a fraction. Small waves sloshed onto a beach somewhere close by. Her reaching feet touched muddy sand. Gradually, the gently sloping sands of a beach came into view, lit by dim, scattered streetlamps. Kali and Amy, shivering uncontrollably, crawled onto dry land, limbs weighted by gravity and fatigue.

For several minutes, Kali knelt numbly on the beach, unable to go on. Her head pounded to the beat of an entire percussion section. She threw up, weakly, retching nothing more than saltwater and bile onto the sand. Tears mingled with the salt on her skin. She fought against the almost overpowering urge to lie down right there and sleep.

No. She couldn't.

They weren't much better off on the beach than in the water. A light breeze sprang up, sucking the last of her body's warmth as it evaporated the water from her skin and underclothes. Mental strength alone got her, still on all fours, up the beach. Reaching a palm tree, she clung to it, hauling herself upright. Her legs barely managed to hold her there.

"C'mon Amy. We have to get our clothes on and find somewhere to stay. We have to get warm." She reached down a hand. With great reluctance, Amy hauled herself upright. Together they struggled into their wet clothes. Kali swayed, her legs trembling. Amy put an arm around her waist and steadied her.

Drawing in great, shuddering breaths, Kali forced her head up. A sign, advertising a beach motel, swam into focus not far away. She shoved herself off the supportive tree and the two took hesitant steps towards the welcoming lights. Sand and grit dug painfully into her water-softened feet.

Bedraggled and sodden, they staggered into the hotel reception office.

The night manager glanced up, bored and sleepy. His expression changed to one of shock and curiosity at the sight of them. Kali leaned heavily on the counter, ignoring the water pooling at her feet.

"Please," she said, her voice an exhausted whisper. "I know we don't look the best but we need a room for the night?"

"Well..." He shifted uncomfortably. "As long as you've got a credit card, I don't see why not. You look like you could use a hot bath, too." He scanned his computer screen and grinned in triumph. "Yep. We even have a room free that has a spa bath. Will that do? A hundred and seventy-five for the night. The breakfast menu is in your room. Just fill out this form, please."

Kali picked up the pen and wrote a fake name with painstaking care. Water blistered the paper and made the ink run.

Amy gave her a despairing look. They had no credit card. Kali pointed significantly at Amy's cleavage. She glanced down, frowning in bemusement, then her pale lips dropped open in an O of comprehension. She turned her back, dragged up her shirt and dug into her bra, audibly ripping at the lining. Pulling several much-folded banknotes from between the padding, she handed them over to the receptionist, along with a sad parody of her usual, flirtatious smile.

He gave her dripping figure the surprised once-over, peeled the soaked US greenbacks apart, hesitated then shrugged. Three hundred US dollars seemed to settle whatever qualms he had. He handed them a room key.

Halfway out the door, Kali paused, clinging to the frame. "Could we get a wakeup call for six am, please?"

The man goggled at her, but nodded and typed something into the computer.

They reached their room and closed the door. Amy wandered into the bathroom and the sound of rushing water followed. Kali leaned against the door for a few minutes, then peeled off her soaked garments and dropped them on the floor. She operated on automatic, now; her last reserves of strength almost gone.

Uncaringly naked, she sank onto the bed and dragged the doona up over her shoulders. She reached for the telephone. With her hand on the handset, she hesitated, trying to push through the haze of brainfry. Was it paranoid to think that maybe Max had Alex's phone tapped? What about Castor's?

Kali dialled a friend's number instead. It was late, but Gav would answer, for sure. She held a quick and fairly cryptic conversation with him, then hung up and waited. Three minutes later the phone rang. Even though she'd been expecting it, she still jumped.

"Caz?"

"Kali! Are you ok? Where are you? Is Amy ok?" Castor was almost incoherent as the questions tumbled off his tongue.

"Caz, just shut up would you?" she said. "Yes, we're both ok. Are we safe on this line?"

"Definitely. Swept every day and scrambled as well. What happened? Where are you?"

"We're in Airlie Beach. It's a long story. We need someone to get us out."

"I've got time. Tell me."

"Well I don't," she snapped back. "Where's Alex?"

"He called in the aborted job, said he was flying to search for Max's boat and has checked in with me every half hour. Actually," there was a pause, "he's due to check in again any minute. He'll need to refuel so I'll send him to the nearest airport and he can collect you two."

"That," Kali yawned, "sounds great. Scramble his line too, though. I'll explain later."

"As soon as I've spoken to him I'm chartering a plane and I'll be there as soon as I can," her brother said severely.

She chuckled but it ended on a sob. "I think we'll be ok here until morning. Let us sleep. It's been a long night."

"I'll call you back once I've heard from Alex." He sounded worried.

"Sure. Thanks Caz." She looked up as Amy emerged from the bathroom, wrapped in a terry robe. She beckoned her over. "Here's someone you ought to talk to."

Handing the phone over to a tearful Amy, Kali shoved herself to her feet, scooped up her wet clothes and staggered to the bathroom. The agony in her head made her dry-retch again, leaning against the wall. Finally she made it into the shower.

She stood for nearly twenty minutes under the sharp hot sting of water, drinking some and half-sobbing in relief as warmth bit into numb toes and feet. At last, she was warm, her skin red, and she found the strength to soap and rinse her clothing and hair. Only with acute reluctance did she finally emerge from the steamy bathroom, bundled in a robe and half-asleep already.

Mechanically, she hung her wet clothes out on the

balcony beside Amy's, before collapsing on the bed. Amy was already fast asleep in the other double bed, her still-wet hair splayed out across the white pillow, tracks of tears showing on her skin, a tissue clutched loosely in her hand.

Kali lay down and reached to pull up the cover when a soft knock at the door brought her wide awake with a rush of adrenalin. Amy slept on. She struggled out of bed and threw the robe back on. Next she palmed a letter opener from the bedside table drawer. Peeking out through the door-spy-hole, she exclaimed aloud at the sight of their visitor.

Opening the door, she ushered Alex in and, once he'd divested himself of two rather mysterious shopping bags, she walked silently into his open arms without a word.

Shuddering with the release of pent up fear, exhaustion and tension, she didn't protest when Alex swept her off her feet and carried her back to the bed. In silence, he pulled down the covers, kicked off his shoes and eased in beside her. Drawing her close against his hard body, he stroked her cheek once and kissed her forehead.

"Go to sleep," he murmured into her ear. "Relax, Kali. I'll take it from here."

"But-"

"No 'but's." He laid a finger on her lips. "There's nothing that won't keep until morning. I've got you. You're both safe. Sleep."

Sighing, she let the tension drain from her shoulders and closed her eyes. It felt good to be secure. Exhausted, head throbbing and body aching, she slept.

*****

A hideously short time later the strident buzzing of the room phone woke her. Hauling herself upright, Kali picked up the handset, listened to a computerised wakeup message then put it down. Every bodily instinct told her to lie back down and sleep but she couldn't. Dawnlight filtered in around the edges of the thick, fish-patterned curtains.

Max's men would discover pretty soon that they'd escaped, if they hadn't already. This little community would be searched. They had to get out.

Rolling over, she looked into Alex's grave, shadowed eyes and smiled in relief.

"I thought you being here might have been a dream."

"You have no idea how much I'm glad it wasn't. You look tired." He reached out and, with a gentle finger, traced the circles that must be under her eyes.

"Thanks," she replied, scraping still-damp hair off her face and wincing as her fingers touched the lump on the back of her head. At least the headache had dulled to a distant, dark throbbing. "That helps, really. I had a rough day."

His air of calm vanished, barely-controlled anger darkening his eyes. "I know. I'm sorry."

She flipped a hand at him and screwed up her nose. "My own dumb fault. I wasn't expecting him to know what was going on, so I wasn't prepared. Violated my own rule - never assume."

His lips thinned and he shook his head but he refrained from saying anything. She was glad. They'd never get anything done if they spent too long laying blame. Mental self-flagellation haunted his expression. He didn't need to voice it.

"Tell me what happened," he said.

Chapter Sixteen

As succinctly and unemotionally as possible, she laid it out for him: The kidnapping, their escape, what Max intended and knew. When she was done, the black expression deepened and Alex slid off the bed. He paced, running a hand through his hair. It was the most agitated she'd ever seen him. He looked over at Amy, who yet slept in the other bed.

"The whole damned thing was a setup?"

She nodded. He swore and resumed pacing.

"Amy and I figure he must have recognised you, and maybe tracked Caz, - probably from a photo your sister carried in her purse or phone. I know you tried to keep your face off the media circuit, but I did see a few shots that showed you clearly. What do you think?"

He stopped. He swore again, long and creatively, his face grim and pale.

"You're right. I can't believe that never occurred to me. I'm an absolute idiot. I've wasted five years and put you two in an appalling situation for absolutely nothing!" He sank onto the bed, holding his head in his hands. "Shit."

Hesitating, unsure of how he'd react, she moved over and sat beside him.

"Can I make a suggestion?"

He laughed harshly. "Go ahead. You can only do

better than my efforts."

"First up," she reached across and turned his face toward her, horrified at the depths of despair in his aspect. Swallowing, she stared at him straitly, "stop wallowing. You're better than this. It's a setback but we'll come up with something."

He stilled then settled into chilly calm. He nodded once, eyes cold. He didn't seem to be angry at her but at himself, and controlling it with an iron will. Hopefully he could keep that control. She needed him thinking straight for both of them.

"Next," she continued, "we need to set up a trap for Max."

A swift frown snapped his brows together and he straightened, jerking away from her. "What?"

She tilted her head to one side. "Max strikes me as the type who doesn't give up easily and who hates to be crossed - especially by women. He will *not* be happy that we've escaped. He'll've found us gone by now, so there's a pretty reasonable chance he'll come here to hunt for us."

Alex opened his mouth, then shut it and gazed off into the distance for awhile. Distaste twisted his mouth.

"You could be right there. Any half sane person would bolt to international waters on the belief that you'd've gone to the police. Max is someone who believes he has all the power. He's so used to dealing with the corruption in southeast Asia that he may well be confident he can pay the police off and take you back again. Let me think."

Torn between annoyance at having control of the situation wrested from her and relief that it had been, Kali used the opportunity to go the bathroom and wake Amy. She protested sleepily, blinked in uncomprehending surprise at Alex and eventually tottered off to the bathroom. Kali went out to the tiny, tiled verandah and pulled their clothes off the railing. They were still damp. She fingered them with distaste.

Alex rose from the bed and fetched the bags he'd brought the night before.

"Some of these will come in handy." He dumped the bags on the bed and tipped one out. "I didn't have time to get your things from the island, so I picked up a few bits and pieces from a late night store here. It was a bit touristy."

She rummaged through the contents. "Hair colour? Spray tan? What the?" She held up a bottle.

"The red dye's for Amy," he said.

"I'm not dying my hair red!" The vibrant blonde protested, emerging from the bathroom. She snatched up a vivid blue blouse and held it to her shoulders. "I like this, though."

"Yes, you are," he said brusquely. "Caz is flying in this morning with a team. He's going to take you back to Brisbane and you're going to get a brand, shiny new life."

"What!?" Amy balled up the shirt and threw it to the bed. "No damned way! I've spent *too* long working my ass off to get where I am. I'm on the verge of a career breakthrough. I'll be famous. I am *not* dying my hair and becoming a...a nobody. It's *your* fault we're in this situation. *You* fix it!"

"*Amy!*" Kali checked Alex, appalled by her friend's bluntness.

His jaw worked but he didn't respond to her accusation. Instead he turned cold scorn on Amy. "Suit yourself. I give you about three days before Max finds you, kidnaps you again and sells you off to his mates in the middle-east out of sheer revenge. Your choice."

Amy gaped at him, her hands balling into fists. She made a noise of absolute frustration, snatched up the dye and the clothing and stalked into the bathroom.

A small smile twitched his lips and he softened as he eyed Kali. "What about you?"

She held up a container of blonde dye. "I'm not

exactly famous."

"Blondes do have more fun, apparently."

"What are you planning, Alex?" She tossed the box aside and put her hands on her hips.

He paused for a moment then scrubbed a hand over his chin and shook his head. "Amy's right: this is my fault and I want you two out of the way. Caz's team can help me take Max when he gets into port. They'll arrest him and we'll take it from there."

She lifted her chin. "You know as well as I do that kidnapping charges are not enough to keep someone like him in jail. He'll claim it was a prewedding cruise or something and it will be our word against his. People saw us go onto the boat willingly. We'll be shredded in court and he'll go free. You need something stronger and you know it."

"Dammit, Kali," he snarled. "Just get somewhere safe and leave this to me, would you? I don't want to have to worry about you."

She cocked her head and eyed him cynically. "Stop playing the hero, Alex. You know you need my help. I can get what you need."

He scowled. "What do you mean?"

"I mean," she set her jaw, "I know where his laptop is. It's on that boat. I saw it in his cabin. There's a safe in the room. The door was open. Looked like he'd just put it back and hadn't shut the door yet. I didn't have time to search it and had no way to keep it dry or I'd've taken it with me. Get me back into his cabin and I'll get the laptop for you."

Alex swung away, resuming his agitated pacing. "No! No way. It's too risky. If he caught you this time he'd just kill you. No, we'll do this the right way. We'll get Caz to get a search warrant. Otherwise the evidence will be inadmissable anyway."

"Didn't seem to worry you last time," she remarked.

"And, if I recall, the anti-terrorism laws give Caz pretty broad powers in situations like this. Besides, if we do it right, Caz will have a good reason to get on the boat without a search warrant. I'll just make sure the laptop is in plain sight when you both come heroically bursting in."

"Last time I didn't have-" he stopped, snapping his teeth together and glaring at her. "Dammit Kali, just don't, please. Amy is safe. Caz will look after her. Just go home and let me finish this."

She drew a long slow breath, walked over to him and took his hands in hers. "Alex, you're going to have to trust me. I know you think this is all on you; all your fault; all your thing to fix. It's not. You need help. I know what to do and you know I'm the only one who can get what you need. Let me get back onto that boat. Let me secure the laptop or make a backup or just distract Max while you get the officials involved. Whatever." She stood on tiptoe and kissed him lightly on the lips.

His fingers gripped hers painfully and he pulled her close for a moment, deepening the kiss, tasting almost of desperation and anger. Then he thrust her away with an oath.

His phone rang. He answered it and became involved in long discussion with Castor about the situation. He looked often at Kali, frowning, arguing with Castor about the pros and cons of her idea until, eventually, his shoulders dropped and he sighed an agreement.

Amy pranced back into the room at that moment and Kali was distracted.

"Wow!" She left Alex to inspect Amy as her friend twirled in front of a mirror. "Your hair looks amazing!"

Amy patted her short, newly-chopped red hair and beamed. "My hairdresser will have a fit but I actually love it, don't you? Is the back tidy enough?"

Kali blinked, not sure what to say. There was no way anyone would recognise Amy. Instead of her usual sleek, elegant hair, sophisticated clothing and subtle makeup, she now sported a funky unbalanced bob, wore a tight black miniskirt and shiny blue halterneck top. She'd also done something to her eyes that made them huge and dramatically blue.

"You definitely won't be recognised, Ames, but take my advice and don't go out at night like that."

"Hundred bucks an hour?" Amy primped in the mirror again.

"At least." It was an old joke between them, from their early teens when Amy used to dress Kali up like a barbie doll and practice the latest makeup styles on her.

A discreet knock brought the conversation up short. Amy clutched at Kali's arm, glancing apprehensively at the door.

"Max wouldn't knock," Alex said drily. He peered out the spy hole, reached for the handle and pulled it open. "Caz. Good to see you."

Kali took a step but Amy shouldered her aside and flung herself into Castor's arms with a cry of delight that quickly dissolved into an incomprehensible sobbed confession. Castor, after an initial confused look at his sister, held Amy close and stroked her bright hair, murmuring reassurances. He led her out onto the back verandah and sat her down on a plastic deck chair, her head pillowed on his shoulder.

Kali wrapped her arms around herself, left out by her best friends for the first time in her life.

"You've done a good thing there, Kali." Alex's deep voice sounded over her shoulder. "He's loved her for years."

"Yes." She strode over to the kitchenette. "So I understand. Tea? Coffee?"

"What's wrong?" He appeared next to her and leaned against the kitchen cupboard, hands shoved into his pockets.

"It doesn't matter." She waved his question away and rested her hands on the bench, head hanging.

She was just tired and being silly. She drove the first wedges between herself and her twin years ago when she'd let Rick dictate how much time she spent with him and with Amy. Castor's secrecy about his job, Amy's decision to settle for a mercenary relationship with Max, her own inability to stick with a relationship, even their current situation with Max - it all came back onto her. She now reaped what she'd sewn years ago. The time had come to repair past mistakes.

She shoved off the bench and, with a look at Castor and Amy still deeply involved in conversation on the verandah, brushed down her robe with sharp, decisive movements.

"I know how to play this, Alex," she returned his quizzical stare with a clear one of her own, "but I'm going to need your help and Castor's. And we need to be quick."

*****

Shivering, Kali spat saltwater as the boat bore down on her. It had throttled back as soon as they'd spotted her. She'd switched on the replacement little gps tracker stitched back into the life vest as soon as Castor and Alex had dropped her into the water, but even half an hour back in the cold sapped her strength. She was actually relieved when the little runabout launched from the back of Max's yacht and came for her.

It wasn't hard to cry and protest weakly as two goons dragged her into the boat - especially when they cracked her head against the side and set fire to her brain again.

Being found in the ocean, rather than on land, meant she couldn't have contacted anyone. She'd been the one to propose it. But right now, shivering and soaked in the bottom of the runabout, with a gun trained on her head, she regretted the choice. Only the memory of Amy, glowing and happy in Castor's embrace, sustained her.

"Where's Amy?" one of the men demanded, pushing the gun muzzle against her head.

Kali allowed her lower lip to tremble. "She...she didn't make it. I lost her in the water and I...couldn't find her again. I don't know where she is. She wasn't a good swimmer. She's...." She broke off, tears obscuring her vision.

"Why did you switch on the tracker?" He shoved the gun barrel against her temple.

She gasped. "I didn't. I didn't know there was one. I was just trying everything. I can't...I'm so tired... please." She let tears fall and curled into a ball, sobbing, watching through her fingers.

The first guard jerked his chin at his fellow who pulled out a radio and spoke in quick Mandarin into it. Her story was explained, questioned and, at last, accepted as they bounced across the water back to the yacht.

The dive board on the stern lowered and the two guards hustled her out of the runabout, arms tightly held. It took bloody-minded determination not to break free. Kali allowed them to drag her; allowed them to leer and joke in Mandarin about the fate that awaited her; allowed them to dig bruises into her arms and pretended to be afraid.

In actuality, her stomach now burned with anger. Any doubts she'd had about Max and his moral standards had well and truly evaporated. Any fears about the consequences of her actions now disappeared as well. This ended today.

They shoved her onto the yacht and half-dragged her downstairs. This time, instead of putting her into a crew cabin, they manhandled her into the main stateroom - Max's cabin. She struggled, for appearances sake, but didn't resist too hard. She couldn't afford to be knocked unconscious again.

As soon as the door closed behind her, Kali tested the handle. Locked and, by the sound of the heavy breathing outside, guarded as well. She studied the deck hatch - closed and, she assumed, locked. A check showed the anchor room was now locked. The four portholes were too small and that about covered all the exits. The bathroom had thin, folding accordion-style doors and offered no hiding places.

Grabbing a chair, she shoved it under the doorhandle. It might buy a few extra seconds anyway. Swallowing down nausea caused by the renewed headache, and forcing her exhausted body to move, she headed straight for the safe, tucked behind its conventional hinged painting on the wall above the desk. It wasn't even a good painting. An ugly Klimt ripoff with too much gold leaf.

Swinging the painting open, she contemplated the keypad of the closed safe. She pulled out the padding of one side of her bra. Unwrapping the tiny electronic device from its waterproof packing she peeled off the cover on the double-sided tape and pressed the gadget onto the safe door, next to the keypad. Finally she pushed the button on the side of the black device and stepped back, waiting. Little green lights flashed vigorously. She cast an anxious look at the door as time dragged on. At last, with a soft *click* the lock opened.

Out of the other side of her bra she tugged a small usb key and unwrapped it. Opening the safe door with delicate fingertips, she withdrew the laptop inside and placed it on the desk. She lifted the lid, tapping her fingers in a rapid staccato as it powered up. Finally, the password window glowed and she plugged the usb device in. Tucking the laptop into a half-open drawer of the desk, she shut the safe door and the picture, wiping away traces of sticky residue on the lock as best she could.

She ran to the starboard side porthole and peered out. Opening it she threw the lock-opening gadget out and waved a hand. With a half-sob of relief, she slid down again and rested her back against the curving wall for a moment. She pressed at her temples with hot, sticky palms and blew a shaky breath.

The door handle rattled.

She swore. It wasn't over yet.

Pushing herself up she stiffened jelly knees and swallowed.

Someone barked orders in Mandarin. The door shuddered. Dammit. A check out the porthole showed they were too soon. Double dammit. She edged away from the porthole, misliking the fact there was nowhere to go except the bathroom, with its flimsy door. She needed a weapon.

The door flew open, the chair splintering under the weight of a burly guard who shouldered it. Max stood behind him, expression disdainful. He stepped inside and shut the door behind him.

"So here we are again, my dear Kalisa," he said, stroking a hand down the sleeve of his blue, silk business shirt. "As you can no doubt feel, we are turning around. So," he gestured at the destroyed chair, "you ruined a perfectly good chair for no reason. There's nowhere to hide and no way to escape this time."

The engines thrummed underfoot and she shifted her weight to stay upright as the boat picked up speed. She resisted the urge to glance at the porthole.

"You may as well relax, dear girl. We have a long trip ahead of us." Max sat down on the edge of the bed and patted the smooth, black silk duvet. Delicate pink cherry blossoms shone beneath his fingers. "You're soaked. Let's get you into a warm shower and a change of clothes." He waved a hand toward the bathroom.

"Where..." she swallowed, not finding it too hard to feign fear, "are you taking me?"

He smiled. "To Thailand as I planned. You have been pre-sold to a buyer who will appreciate your...charms." He gave a false sigh of regret. "It is a pity. I will have to give him a refund for Amy, though. Is she really dead?"

She covered her mouth and closed her eyes. "We got separated in the water. She drowned. She... she was your fiance! How can you be so... horrible?!"

He looked supremely uninterested. "Surely your friend Alex has told you his sad tale of woe; his reason for pursuing me so relentlessly for the last five years."

There was no point in denying it. She nodded wordlessly, shivering with more than just cold.

"Amy was simply a means to an end." He pursed his lips and inspected her, his eyes drifting the length of her body until she felt underdressed. "I needed to get through her to your brother and thence to Alex. I needed him off my back. He was getting too close."

Kali gasped, unable to believe his admission even though she'd already suspected it all. "So you... you're telling me his story is true? You had his sister and brother-in-law killed?"

He shrugged, apparently indifferent. "They were at the wrong place at the wrong time. It was unfortunate, but that's how things go sometimes. If he hadn't tried to escape, they may have even survived to be ransomed."

Max stood, tossing aside a cushion he'd been stroking methodically. He took two steps closer. She backed away until she hit a wall and could go no further. He reached out and ran his fingertips down her cheek.

It took every ounce of self-restraint she possessed not to drive an elbow into his complacent face and break his jaw. She needed to buy time and if he cried out or overpowered her the guards could come back, and the laptop could be discovered. Distracting Max, not damaging him, had to be the path – unfortunately.

"Castor and Alex will come for me," she whispered, trying not to shake.

She had this. She could do this.

Nausea twisted her stomach.

"I know," he murmured, leaning closer, his breath brushing her skin. "I'm counting on it. But," he straightened and reached down and took hold of her wrist, "since we've disabled our gps tracking unit, they won't know where you are until I switch it back on. So we'll be well out of Australian waters, by the time they catch up with us, and perfectly safe. Or at least," his smile was cool, "I'll be perfectly safe. Then," he ran a hand over her wet hair, "I can give them a sea-burial and scuttle their vessel. It will be months, if ever, before it's found and by then it will be far too late for you."

Chapter Seventeen

Max grabbed Kali and threw her bodily onto the wide bed. She hit the mattress and rolled back over one shoulder to land on her feet on the floor on the other side. The room swam and she reached for a wall to steady herself.

"Enough." He pulled a small pistol out of his pocket and pointed it at her. "I'm not interested in chasing you around the room. Maybe some other time. For now, get on the bed." He extracted two pairs of handcuffs from a side drawer and tossed one of them to her. "We have unfinished business, you and I."

She caught and weighed them in her hand, eyeing Max's smug smile distastefully. Alex and the others needed more time. What choice did she have? Shit.

She climbed onto the bed and secured one loop to a ring set into the wall over the middle. The open cuff went around her left wrist, loosely. Max waved the gun. She gritted her teeth and tightened the cuff.

"Better. Now the other one." He flicked the second pair of cuffs onto the bed.

Slowly, she lifted them over her head, attaching them to the ring and to her right wrist, hating the sick, fluttery fear threatening to choke her throat and mind. Obedience came with dark memories and an upwelling of old, helpless anger so consuming it almost obliterated free thought.

No. This was not Rick. She was not helpless and

powerless in his control. Scooting her backside closer to the wall, she tried not to let a spasm of relief show. The cuffs bit deep into her wrists but she could reach her hair.

"Now." He laid the gun down and reached for his clothing, tugging the blue silk shirt free of his pants.

She swallowed hard, struggling to keep her head. Think. She had to think. Dammit, why was her brain so mushy? She was in control, not him. Forcing her mind off the dark path of fear, she fumbled in her wet hair with cold fingers. There. It was the work of moments to pull the bobbypin free, bend it open and pull off one plastic tip.

Max unbuckled his belt.

She needed a little more time. Her fingers shook with fear and adrenalin. She was out of practice. The pin slipped between sweaty fingertips.

He unzipped his pants.

"Seriously?" She raised her chin and one eyebrow as her fingers felt the lock and slid the pin in. "You're really going to play the sleazy badguy routine?" She managed a contemptuous sneer.

He paused, smirking slightly. "Only as much as you'll play the plucky heroine, but since there's no eleventh hour rescue for you, I suspect it won't last long. Such games bore me, anyway. I've always found you more attractive than Amy, but I'd prefer it if you shut up now."

Levering sideways produced the soft click of release and she almost cried out in relief.

He moved closer.

Keeping her hands where they were, she worked on the other lock. The metal bit painfully into her wrists. Then it, too clicked free. Thank God for Castor, his childhood obsession with spy movies.

"I'm sure you would prefer quiet," she bent one knee up, trying to get purchase with her foot on the slippery material of the bedcover, "but I'm going to disappoint you there. I'm not some broken, terrified little girl too scared to resist. I will *not* make it easy. Believe me, you *really* don't want to do this." She swallowed and clenched her teeth as he gave her an ironic, sympathetic smile.

He uttered a short, unamused laugh, dropped his pants to the floor and climbed onto the bed. His cold hands came to rest on her ankles and began a slow slide up her calves.

He shoved at her raised knee, pushing her leg wide.

"Oh yes," he murmured, "I really do. Go ahead. Resist."

She shuddered but forced herself to stay still. Just another few centimetres.

She waited until his face was just inches from hers, one hand resting on her out-turned thigh, the other holding his weight on the bed.

Then she moved.

One shin went into his groin. An elbow knocked his arm out from beneath him. A shove flipped him into a curled, howling ball of pain. She slid behind him until she got an arm around his neck, cutting off gargled cries for help. He gasped and thrashed, trying to grab her, snagging her hair. She gritted her teeth. Instead of letting go as he pulled harder, she tightened the stranglehold and held on. Tears blurred her vision as he wrenched at her hair. Shifting her weight, she shoved a knee into his back and arched away. His grip relaxed and he let go.

His struggles weakened. His fingers scrabbled at her arm, nails scraping deep into skin.

The door burst open. Max's men exploded into the room, guns drawn, faces frightened, yelling about a boat approaching. They saw Kali and aimed. She let the strangle hold go in order to duck behind the scant protection of Max's body. His arms waved feebly and he rolled away, croaking an order at his men.

"Kill her. Now."

Shit.

She dropped off the side of the bed as two bullets tore

into the mattress. Heavy footsteps sounded. She tucked her feet under and came into a crouch, ready to leap even though there was nowhere to go. One of the men loomed over her. Max appeared beside him, his face red with anger and trapped blood. He massaged his throat, threw her one sneering, contemptuous look then flicked a hand at his man.

"Do it."

The gun-finger squeezed. She dove to one side, curling to roll to her feet. The shot slapped into the wall behind. The gun swung toward her again, centring on her chest, less than a foot away this time. No way to escape.

She didn't even try. She reached over the top with one hand; beneath with the other. She grabbed and pushed up. The gun went off, over her head; deafening; splintering the timber ceiling. A sharp twist of his wrist loosened his grip. Turning it back toward its owner she wrenched it free.

Now it was in her hand, pointed at him. She stepped out of reach.

The man's eyes widened and he took a half-step backward.

"Shoot her!" Max's voice slid up half an octave as he glared at his second guard.

Kali stepped back further. She aimed the gun toward Max, but looked at his armed guard.

"I guarantee I can get one shot off," she said. "So what's it going to be?" Her hand quivered. She sucked a deep breath, trying settle the adrenalin-shakes.

The man hesitated, glancing toward his boss. Max sneered.

"Shoot her. She doesn't have what it takes."

The guard's finger shifted. She launched herself sideways, squeezing the trigger at the same time. The shots rang out at almost simultaneously. Glass shattered somewhere behind her. Two more shots immediately followed, though she hadn't pulled the trigger again.

Something slammed into her thigh. Had she been shot? No pain followed. She hit the ground hard, barely hanging onto the gun as her hand smacked into a table and her shoulder took the brunt of the fall. She curled her head in, trying to protect it against another drubbing. A heavy weight pinned her legs. Max's man lay across her. His brown eyes stared starkly back at her.

She looked up, raising the gun toward Max, determined to end it. Whatever the consequence to herself, this had to finish. Now.

Max remained upright, hands at shoulder height, scowling at someone who stood at the door, out of Kali's sight. A stain, spreading dark across the blue silk of his shirt, was testament to her shot. She'd missed his heart. The bullet must've passed straight through his side, about a handspan too low. The best possible outcome was a punctured bowel. Maybe he'd die of peritonitis. That was a pleasant thought. It sounded like a drawn out and painful death.

She bit down on the hysterical giggle bubbling behind her lips.

"Kali, you ok?"

Her heart leapt.

Alex.

"Yes." Finding her voice, she wriggled out from beneath the body.

There wasn't anything more that could be said, here and now, without releasing a floodgate of emotion. This was not the time.

A quick check showed no injury to her leg, just a thick smear of glistening blood from the guard. She pushed into a sitting position, with her back against the curved hull and the gun still trained on Max. Alex stood in the doorway, a black frown pulling at his brows; his finger curled around the trigger of a pistol aimed at Max's head; his body tense and poised.

"Don't, Alex," she said. "Leave him to Caz. Don't ruin your life. Please?"

He inspected her swiftly then, apparently satisfied, jerked his chin at Max. His hard expression didn't change.

"Did he do anything to you?" His eyes glittered with anticipation, as though he just awaited an immediate reason to pull the trigger.

She laughed a little breathlessly. "Nothing I couldn't handle." Another shrewd look from him made her smile faintly back. "I'll be fine, Alex. Let's just get this over with. Don't kill him. For Shelley."

He turned a level gaze on Max and gestured with the gun. "Put your pants on, you look like an idiot." His shoulders relaxed a fraction, scorn replacing the implacable anger.

Scowling, Max dragged his clothing on and stalked out into the hallway, anger almost visibly steaming from him. Blood seeped through his fingers where he had them clamped around the wound on his side. Alex followed, gun unwaveringly trained on Max's back.

Kali struggled to her feet and staggered after them.

Up on deck, Castor had things well in hand, his men having subdued the crew and taken their places running the boat. The ship swayed and shifted as the new captain reversed their course, back toward shore. Nearby, a Coast Guard boat shadowed her every move.

Alex shoved Max over to join his crew where Castor's men had them all huddled together in preparation for taking them onto the Coast Guard boat. The two boats slowed and, calm water making it relatively easy, the transfer began.

Kali, conscious of Max's penetrating, stolid glare, left the bright sunshine and sought refuge in the elegant dining area belowdecks. She curled up on a leather-upholstered seat and wrapped her arms around her knees, staring out over the sparkling blue ocean.

"You ok?"

She jumped, gun raised defensively, then relaxed marginally as Alex's lean form came into view. Her hands shook and she clenched them tightly around the butt of the gun to stop it. His warm fingers wrapped around hers. He gently tugged the gun free and flicked the safety on, laying it down on a coffee table. His arm, bearing a blanket, went around her shoulder. He wrapped her up and drew her against his body, one hand stroking her hair.

"It's ok, Kali. It's over. You were absolutely amazing."

She drew a deep breath, willing her body to relax. She uncurled a little and looked up at him through her lashes.

"You did get what you needed, didn't you? From the laptop?"

He hesitated, with something akin to surprise in his eyes. "Yes, Lacey found what we needed. She hacked in wirelessly from the other yacht when you connected her up, then called Caz in with the Coast Guard boat when she had it all. You left the laptop where Caz's men found it easily, too."

"And it's enough to convict him do you think?" She squeezed her hands into fists. The pain of her fingernails biting into her palms was almost enough to distract her from the fire in her skull; and the memories - for the moment. Later, who knew.

Alex's mouth thinned into a wintry, satisfied smile. "Oh yes. Lacey says it looks like records of all his drug movements, his people, his workshops, his suppliers...even...the name of the man who bought you and Amy."

She shuddered and stood up, pacing the length of the room and back again, holding the blanket tightly wrapped around herself.

"I saw the handcuffs," he said conversationally, "and the marks on your wrists. How did you get free?"

She inspected her hands. Red bands marked where the cuffs had tightened against her flesh. Livid, bloody scratches from Max's nails stood out against her pale skin. She flashed Alex a swift, false smile.

"A bobby pin and the legacy of playing spy with Caz as a kid. Easy." She scrubbed the heels of her palms over her face. "It was the gun to my head and the order to kill me I'm struggling with."

He stood and strode to her side, taking her hands in his and stroking her bruised wrists with his thumbs.

"I know. Believe me, I know, Kali." With care and extreme gentleness, he pulled her close and held her against his chest. "I don't think....no, never mind," he murmured, his lips against her hair.

Kali opened her mouth to ask what he'd been going to say.

Three quick gunshots rang out abovedecks.

Alex swore, shoved her aside and ran up the short staircase onto the deck. Kali picked up the gun and followed, more slowly. She peered around the doorframe, gun ready, safety off.

Sprawled on the deck, Max stared emptily at the blue sky. Dead. Two shots neatly drilled through his heart. Blood spread on the polished timber deck, brilliant red in the tropical glare.

"Castor!" She gazed in horror at her brother.

He sat on the deck, pale and blood-spattered, holding his right leg. Blood dripped to the deck beneath him. One of his men ripped a shirt and bound the injury. Castor sent her an exasperated, worried look.

"I'm fine, Kali. Bastard grabbed a gun and got one off before I could shoot. It missed everything vital. Just hurts like you wouldn't believe. Ow!" He snarled at the man binding his leg.

She dropped to the deck beside him and threw her arms around him. He held her awkwardly, patting her back, ordering someone to take the gun from her before he got shot again. Unbidden, tears gathered and fell, obscuring her vision. Sniffing, she wiped at the tears with the heel of a hand and sat back on her haunches. He regarded her apprehensively. She gave a watery laugh. He'd never been any good handling upset women, except Amy. Kali kissed him on the cheek and stood back as the paramedics carried him to the other boat.

Alex stood over the corpse, staring pensively down at the blank eyes. She came up beside him and slipped a hand into his. He squeezed her fingers but didn't say anything and she stayed silent, respecting his need to find closure.

Castor's men took photographs. The paramedics came and manhandled the body into a black bodybag, zipping away without ceremony the man who made Alex into what he was today; who had played puppeteer to all of them the last few days and longer.

When it was gone, only emptiness and a lingering sense of horror, remained. She expected there would be nightmares in the coming weeks. Therapy would be a good idea. Later. When it all started to sink in. Right now she felt nothing and could barely stand or think straight as the adrenalin ebbed and left her thick-headed and clumsy.

Finally, it was her turn to leave the boat and she clambered down and across to the Coast Guard ship. Alex caught her when her foot slipped on the ladder, his arms strong and sure. He looped an arm under hers and held her up when she staggered on the shifting deck of the Coast Guard vessel. Her feet didn't seem to belong to her, so she leaned on him, dazed.

When the last of the returning crew were aboard, with only a skeleton group left to sail Max's boat back to harbour, the Coast Guard captain gunned his engines and sped off, outstripping the yacht and flying over the water. Wrapped in a dry jacket, Kali perched out on the bow, eyes watering from the sting of salt, wind and emotion.

Everyone left her alone, and she was fine with that. Alex joined her after awhile and tried to talk to her, but her throat was too tight to speak and, eventually, he lapsed into silence and simply sat beside her.

Once back at harbour, there followed a confusing couple of hours during which she made statements to Castor's people, the local police and the federal police. She got tired of repeating the story. It didn't make sense any more, anyway. Why on earth had she offered to go back on the boat? Who the hell knew? Her brain was fuzzy with exhaustion, throbbing pain and the aftermath of adrenalin. Her words slurred and the room washed into an abstract painting without edges or shape. She tried to stand, only to find her legs wouldn't obey.

Some sort of argument went on over her head. It made no sense either so she stopped trying to follow it as her eyes closed of their own accord. The blurred world vanished. Someone picked her up and carried her somewhere quiet. Alex. His warm scent filled her nostrils. Her cheek rested on his shoulder. She allowed herself to relax.

Chapter Eighteen

Kali woke with a gasp of fear, sitting up in a familiar, yet unfamiliar bed. Flinging the covers aside she stood on bare, shaky legs, trying to work out where she was. She wore a tshirt and underwear but nothing else. The room was softly lit. Grey light crept in around the edges of thick blinds. Dawn light? Turning in a circle she tried to slough off the remnants of a nightmare she didn't want to even think about; tried to get her brain to connect the dots and tell her where she was.

Her own room. Her house. Brisbane. What the hell? Why was she here? Had it all been a dream? Had she never left? How had she got here?

The other side of the bed was empty but had been slept in. Alex? Where was he now? The house felt empty. Only the kookaburras, laughing in the trees outside, broke the silence.

Her bladder was bursting so she took care of that and changed into clean clothes. She didn't even check in the mirror. Her hair was straw and her skin itched with salt but a shower could wait until she got some answers. At least the headache had faded to a dull, background thudding; bearable, if not enjoyable.

Opening the door to the living room, she got a sense of emptiness there, too. The second bedroom was her office, which explained why, assuming it was Alex, he'd slept in her bed. However it didn't explain where he was now or why he'd left her alone.

Shivering in the unexpected cool, she wandered into the kitchen. She opened the fridge out of habit, but it was empty except for a couple of beers and a packet of withered carrots. The thought of food made her ill, anyway. She closed it again and poured a glass of water, instead. It tasted unpleasantly metallic. She tipped half of it down the sink.

Outside the kitchen window, the grey light of dawn brightened to pinkish yellow and the kookaburras gave one last raucous round of laughter before the chortling died away into road noise and other city sounds.

She hesitated, uncertain what to do.

On the bench lay a folded paper with her name scrawled across it. What was with this man and leaving notes? She opened it.

Had to fly back to the island early this morning to pick up our gear and sort out guests and details for Amy. I'll be back this afternoon. I'll stop in to check on you. Sorry to leave you alone now. Caz called and asked you to call back.

Thankyou.

Alex.

Kali squinted at it and read it again just to let it sink in. That was it? 'Thankyou'? What did that even mean? Thankyou for what?

She groaned. What did she expect: fireworks and the key to his apartment? Protestations of undying gratitude and love? After all, they had an agreement. She'd done her part. Amy was safe. Alex had his revenge. He was free to get on with his life now.

Slowly she folded the paper and put it to one side, unsure of what to feel or think. The events of the last few days seemed surreal and distant. Had she really done all that? Had she risked her life and helped capture Max?

Was he really dead? Amy. How was she?

And Castor!

After a few frantic seconds of searching for her phone, she stopped hunting. Max had taken it from her. She picked up the landline, a relic she never used, and dialled Amy's mobile from memory. It went to voicemail and she hung up in frustration.

She tried Castor's. He answered, sounding sleepy. A look at the clock showed it was almost eight am. It just seemed earlier because the sun hid behind clouds. Had she slept eighteen hours, or a full day and a half? What day was it?

"You ok?" Last she remembered he'd been dripping blood on the deck of the boat. "Where are you?"

"Princess Alexandra Hospital in Brisbane," he yawned his answer. "I'm fine. You?"

"I... I guess." She hesitated, not quite knowing what she felt. A little bit empty maybe. Like something was missing. "Want to fill me in on why I'm here and how I got here? I don't remember much after getting off the boat at Shute Harbour."

He laughed. "I wasn't in much of a position to help. It was all I could manage to keep from being whipped off to hospital the moment we set foot on land. Alex stepped in when the local uniforms gave you the third degree." He gave an ironic chuckle. "My credentials didn't impress them much but he did the bored, rich, don't-fuck-with-me thing perfectly and walked all over them when he saw you were about to pass out. Whisked us away to the jet and brought us both back to Brisbane. Took you home, I gather. What, is he not there?"

"No, he left a note saying he'd gone back to the island to sort out the guests and details for Amy. Said he'd be back this afternoon. Caz are you sure you're ok? What'd the doctor say?"

"I'm fine, worry-wort," he assured her. "All stitched

up and healing nicely. Through and through muscle only. Couple of weeks of physio and I'll be back on deck. Apparently I'm not as good at getting out of the way of bullets as you are." His grin was almost audible. "Alex tells me you dodged Matrix-style. Sweet. Told you we need you on board. We'd make a good team."

Kali sucked a shuddering breath and made an involuntary gesture to push his words, and her memories, away.

"Don't."

"Hey!" He sounded concerned.

She rushed in, interrupting before he could say anything else about it. "And...Amy?" Were they together? Did she dare ask or what it too early?

He laughed, his whole demeanour changing by the tone of his voice. "She's been here with me all night - just out at the moment. I think..." he stopped and awe seeped into his voice. "I think there might be a chance for us. Don't want to jinx it though, so don't gossip with her about me, please?"

She wiped away inexplicable tears with the tip of one finger. "No, I wouldn't. I love you both too much to ruin it for you. Just be patient with her, will you?" Her throat was tight and she raised her face toward the ceiling in an effort to loosen it and prevent more tears falling. What was wrong with her?

"Me? Of course!" He chuckled. "I am the soul of patience."

"Right, sure." She smiled and sniffed. "Well, I guess I'll try and get back to some sort of normality. Seems weird though."

There was a short silence then Castor spoke up again, sounding a little more subdued. "Kali, you went through a lot yesterday. Maybe you should give yourself a little time. Talk to a professional. I can send the psych from the department over, if you like."

"No!" She rejected the idea more forcefully than she meant to and softened her tone. "No, not yet Caz. Thanks, but I'll be fine. What happened yesterday..." she shivered with recollection. "It wasn't nice but it was short and really, compared to what Rick put me through, not unbearable. I wasn't helpless. At least, not entirely. I'll get over it." Tears gathered again, spilled and slid down her cheeks. Breath caught in her lungs. Appalled at herself, she hastily snatched at a tissue and tried to breathe quietly.

"And what about Alex?" Castor dropped the question into the silence.

"What about him?" She paced a few steps toward the front door then back into the loungeroom. Her head started to pound again. She fingered the bruises on the back of her skull, wincing.

"Has he talked to you at all since?"

She snorted. "You saw me yesterday. I was doing well to string two words together and he left before I woke up today, so: no."

There was another long pause. What was he hedging around? Normally he was hard to shut up.

"He's a good guy, Kali. Did I tell you how we met?"

"No." She sank onto a couch. Clearly this would be a longer conversation than she'd anticipated. "Is it important right now?" She rested her forehead on the heel of her hand and closed her eyes.

He drew a breath and let it gust out. "Yes, I think it is, actually. He used to be with the SAS. And he is a chemical engineer. I met him a year or so after I was recruited to ASIS. He was one of the trainers. It was about the same time that you hooked up with Rick and we hardly saw each other."

"Caz, I'm sor-" she began, meaning to apologise to her brother, to let him know what an idiot she'd been.

"Forget it." He dismissed it. "I'm the one who should

apologise. I should've looked out for you. I feel bad that I didn't step in and do something. We were both pretty young and, well, you don't have a great track record of listening to me anyway." He chuckled. "Anyway...about the time you ditched Rick, Alex saw a recent photo of us on my desk. He commented about how sad you seemed and I...well...I told him about Rick and what he'd done to you. What I knew, anyway. Sorry."

"What?" Kali sat up straight, gripping a pillow in one fist. "You told a complete stranger about my private life? Oh my God, how humiliating! Why?"

"C'mon. He was a good friend and I needed advice. I didn't know how to help you. He seemed like the appropriate person." Castor sounded exasperated.

She tried to rein in her anger. What the hell was wrong with her? She'd spent years getting her head straight and now, one stupid incident and she was losing the emotional control she'd worked so hard for?

"Why, Caz? Why was he the appropriate person?" she said, weary of the way he was stringing this out.

She pressed a finger into the third eye spot between her brows in an attempt to alleviate the pain.

"Before I tell you that, I need to tell you what he did when I told him how Rick had treated you," her brother added.

"What?" she repeated, feeling stupid and thick-headed. "Why would it matter?"

Castor ignored the question. "Didn't you ever wonder why you never heard from Rick? It's because Alex made sure of it. As soon as he found out, he went in with back up and, well... basically took the guy apart - his life, I mean. Alex'd already built up a substantial business so he had the contacts - although I'm pretty sure he didn't let him get away physically untouched. He basically got the guy bankrupted and kicked out of the country. Rick's working as a construction labourer in New Zealand now. Alex keeps tabs on him, just to make sure. Rick Bowman is incapable of ever hurting you or any other young woman again."

Kali blinked, unable to quite process what he was saying. "Alex did that? Really? But why? I don't understand, Caz. He didn't even know me. And why didn't you tell me? It would've helped to know he was out of the country."

"Alex made me promise not to tell you he'd been involved."

"But *why?*" She groaned, holding her head as the room swam. "Why would he do something like that?"

There was a long silence, then Castor cleared his throat.

"Rick's his half-brother, ok?" He growled down the phone. "Alex Schiffer is Alex Bowman. He felt responsible and did what he could to fix it. He wanted to meet you, to apologise, but before I could get you two together, his sister was killed and he went off the rails a bit. Since then and until now, his whole focus has been on Max. This week brought you two together finally. Give him a break, Kali. He deserves a break."

She didn't know what to say. Alex knew who she was and who Rick was, all along. What did that mean? Had he just seen her as some sort of tool to be used in his revenge scenario? Someone with a history of being easy to manipulate and string along? Did everyone around her have some sort of long term agenda she wasn't aware of? Did they all want to use her to achieve what they wanted? Was she just some sort of serial victim that people like Rick and Max abused?

Could she really have been stupid enough to fall for someone like that again?

Castor asked her a question she didn't understand. She mumbled something and hung up. He called straight back but she didn't answer, just stared at the phone on the side table until it rang out.

It started ringing again. She slowly and deliberately unplugged the cord from the wall and let it fall. The noise stopped.

She tried to stand up, only to find her legs wouldn't support her. Instead she sank back into the cushions and looked blankly at the black TV screen opposite. Had it only been less than a week ago that Castor had told her about Alex and the Ebay sale?

Her head was fuzzy; her thinking stodgy and filled with sharp points of agony. It just didn't make any sense. Christ, why couldn't she think straight?

Forcing herself to stand up, she staggered toward the bathroom, hunting for painkillers - anything to dull the agony in her head and her heart. She didn't make it. Her legs gave way and she fell to her knees on the living room rug, bewildered. Unable to make her body move, Kali slipped sideways and folded to the floor.

*****

Lights flickered overhead. Worried voices filtered through the haze. Movement made her want to throw up. She tried to talk; tried to tell them to stop; shook her head in protest only to cry out in pain. Hands and voices soothed but she couldn't understand them. Was it Max? Had he kidnapped her again? She struggled against the hands but was too weak to break free. Darkness slipped in to drag her away again.

*****

Kali opened sticky eyelids to an unfamiliar ceiling. With uncomprehending senses, she explored her surroundings. Thick, white sheets tucked firmly in, white ceiling, white walls, something beeping irritatingly nearby. Hospital. The word clanked into her mind and rattled around, searching for a reason to connect to.

"Kali!" Amy's worried, beautiful face swam into view. Kali reached up to touch the vibrant red hair, now neatly cut and curled.

"You kept it," she whispered.

"You're ok! She's ok!" Amy looked up at someone entering the room.

Castor swung in on crutches, through the door and to her bedside. He smiled tentatively, holding one of her hands like it was porcelain.

"You had us worried, kid," he said. His green eyes were haunted reflections of her own.

"What happened?" She blinked and rubbed sleep away, her arm surprisingly heavy. There was a drip stuck in her right hand.

"You didn't tell us about the crack Max gave you over the skull." He peered at her. "You have concussion and some swelling of the brain. The medicos have done MRIs and they say it'll go down naturally. You'll be fine, but they're keeping you in for observation until tomorrow."

"What day is it?" Bright morning sunshine streamed through the window.

"Friday." Amy squeezed her hand. "You've been asleep for ages. Part of the problem was that you hadn't eaten for two days either. I'm sorry. I should have told Caz about Max hitting you."

Kali managed a shrug. "I screwed up your wedding, so we can call it evens."

"Mum and Dad've been in," Castor said, patting her hand with awkward sympathy. "They're coming back after lunch."

"Great." She groaned. Explaining things to her mother. What fun. "What about…Alex?"

She caught a look between Amy and Castor.

"He's…" Castor hesitated, "he's caught up with my bosses and with the federal police - giving evidence and helping them with their investigations."

"Caz," she sighed, "even I know that's code for 'he's done something suspicious and they want to question him'.

Do they need more from me?"

Her brother grimaced and jerked his chin toward the door. "There's an officer waiting outside to take your full statement. Apparently you didn't make a lot of sense the other day - not surprising when you consider the head injury. Are you up to it now?"

She hesitated, then nodded. Castor called the officer in and the session started.

She did the best she could. At least, after sleep and whatever they put in her drip she could think straight now. She just kept shoving the emotions aside and coming at it from a purely clinical, logical viewpoint. It was painful. A hollow, lost, sickness churned in the pit of her stomach and swelled in her throat every time she thought or spoke about Alex. The knowledge that he'd just used her to get to Max; that he'd known all along about Rick; that he'd still manipulated and played with her emotions so damned thoroughly that she'd begged him to let her help - it made speaking unemotionally impossible.

She was determined to do the right thing, though. Max had destroyed Alex's family and, even though that didn't make Alex's actions right, it did make them understandable. She stopped frequently to let her throat clear and wipe her eyes. The officer was understanding and patient. Castor and Amy sat, hand in hand, watching her anxiously.

At last, when it was over and she'd signed off on the statement and allowed them to photograph the bruise on the back of her head and the marks on her wrists, they all left and Kali was left alone with her thoughts and a different kind of ache.

Was it possible to feel hate, love, despair, anger and hope all at once?

No. She closed her eyes. It might be possible, but it was stupid. She had to accept that she'd been an idiot, that Alex had used her, and just learn from it. She thought she'd been so damned smart and savvy, but she'd just repeated her old mistake of trusting and loving someone who had only their own interests at heart, not hers.

Tears soaked her pillow.

Doctors and her parents came and fussed. They left and she slept. That was all she could really do, anyway. Medication dulled the ache in her chest as well as the nightmares.

A day later they released her. She went home, numb and operating on automatic.

Chapter Nineteen

A key rattled in the front door. Kali, up to her elbows in dishwater and expecting Castor, called out, "I'm in the kitchen."

She dried her hands and, at the sound of measured footsteps in the hall, spoke again.

"You really don't need to check up on me every day, Caz, and since when do you arrive on time, anyway?"

"Since I'm not him." Alex's deep voice just preceded his appearance around the corner.

Her heart leapt at the sight of his lean form then dropped at the look on this handsome face. His eyes narrowed; his mouth pressed tight. Five swift strides brought him to her side. She lifted her chin, glaring in cold defiance. He stopped, scanned her, then nodded in apparent satisfaction. Clearing his throat, he headed for the couch, hesitated and perched on the arm and gazed at her calmly.

She folded her arms across her chest and stared levelly back. "Why are you here, Alex?"

He shrugged one shoulder, his expression now blank and cool. "We have unfinished business."

She twitched at the echo of Max's words on the boat. Forcing artificial calm onto herself, she raised her brows.

"Oh?" She would *not* let him run the show this time. He'd twisted her around his little finger since the beginning and she'd sworn never to let anyone do that again. She slid from hope to despair, then chose cold anger as the best defence against whatever explanation he chose.

He folded his arms, mirroring her. "You won't return my calls and Caz's telling me to leave you alone. The police outside your hospital room refused me admittance on Friday, so I figured you must be angry with me for some reason. What is it?"

She blinked at him for a moment, trying to work out his angle. Could he be that stupid? Did he think she wouldn't find out? No. Stupid he definitely wasn't; or naive. Castor must have given him the key and would have told him he'd revealed his little secret. Alex wanted something.

"What do you want, Alex?"

She yanked open the fridge. Her hand shook as she poured a glass of orange juice. When she turned around, he stood behind her. He plucked the glass from her hand when she jumped and sloshed juice on the floor.

"Kali, you've had a traumatic experience and you're not over a head injury. First of all I want to make sure you're ok. Then, when I'm sure of that, I want..." he paused and swept a hand through his hair. "I want us." He pointed at her, then at himself. "I want us to work."

It was a good thing he'd taken the glass from her hand or she would have dropped it. She turned away, hardly able to take in what he'd said.

"A.Alex," she stammered, anger and confusion making her tongue thick, "I don't... how can you...you *used* me. You *knew* about Rick and what he'd done and you still thought it was ok to manipulate me into helping you!" She paced the tiny kitchen area, trying to hold herself together and speak calmly.

He opened his mouth. She glared at him and held up a hand. He shut it again, arms still folded across his chest.

"And...making love to me," she growled, hating the

sickness in her stomach, "what was that, pity?"

Why was she even letting him stay in her house?

"No!" He unfolded his arms, paling. "I-"

"Shut up!" She pointed a finger at him. "You don't get to talk yet." When he closed his lips she continued. "There were any number of times you could've told me who you were, but you didn't! You...you tricked me into helping you and then you played on my history; on my need to prove myself...to further your own ends. Who does that?" You had me *begging* you to let me help. You *used* me. I still can't believe what I did for you!"

"Neither could I, Kali." He scraped his fingers through his dark-blond hair.

She put her hand on her hips. "What the hell does that mean? You got me to do *exactly* what you needed."

He stalked forward, glowering.

Fear fluttered low in her stomach as he backed her into a corner of the kitchen and looked straight into her eyes.

"It's my turn now. Hear me out."

She brought up her hands, curling them into loose fists and shifting her feet into a fighting stance. "Back the hell off, Alex, or I'll make you. You don't get to tell me what to do. Not now, not ever."

He flinched away, horror flickering through his grey eyes as he glanced down at her defensive position. Shoving back he put space between them and held up his hands, palm out.

"I'm sorry. I didn't mean to scare you...dammit!" He ran a hand over his face and turned away. Placing his palms on the grey granite benchtop he dropped his head low.

"Hear me out...please, Kali?"

Something in his low, rough words caught her attention. She nodded slowly, lowering her hands.

"I never wanted to put you in the middle of all this. Ask Caz. Knowing your history, I argued against the whole Ebay thing from the start. When it finally came down to the wire and became clear we had no choice, I had to let it happen or lose my chance. So I couldn't tell you who I was. You'd never have agreed to go to the island with Rick Bowman's brother, would you?"

She shook her head in reluctant agreement. Definitely not.

"Especially," he added, "as Caz obviously doesn't know the whole story between you and Rick." His mouth twisted. "What he told me just made it sound like Rick had taken financial and physical advantage of a young girl. He'd done it before so I packed him off to New Zealand as a favour to Caz, more than anything. He was worried about you. If I'd known how bad it was…how much Rick's abuse had affected you…"

He lifted haunted eyes to hers. When she didn't reply and didn't move he continued.

"I also didn't know about Max's interest in you. If you remember, as soon as you told me how you felt about him and I saw how he looked at you, I tried to call the whole thing off."

Now it was his turn to pace the small area of tiled floor. "Dammit, Kali. I did *not* want to put you in harm's way. It never occurred to me you would be in any real danger. I've been beating myself over the head for missing something so freaking obvious as a photo."

He sucked in a long, slow breath and came back to stand in front of her, his expression troubled, full of such pain and fear that she reached a hand out. He caught it and laid it along his cheek, softening to worry.

"It wasn't until I saw how close I'd come to losing you on that boat; how strong you were; how cool - that I realised what my obsession with getting Max almost cost me. I lost my sister, Kali. Losing you would've been…just as bad. But you were so damned determined to help with Max and I was so afraid he'd never leave you alone…" He searched her face. "I couldn't think of any other way for you to be free, other than to put you back in danger. I'm sorry."

She said nothing, unable to put into words the tumult of emotion roiling in her heart. Wanting to believe him, but not willing to. He'd used her.

"But," he closed his eyes for a second and put her hand gently away, "I understand that you must hate me for who I am and the position I put you in. I don't blame you. I hate myself. So I just came to find out if you're ok. Tell me you're ok, Kali and I'll leave you alone."

Turning her back, so he wouldn't see the gathering of angry tears she couldn't stop, Kali quickly wiped them away and gazed out over the lush green back lawn. Was she ok? She'd successfully fought back from Rick's mindgames on her own - at least she thought she'd been successful. A few recent realisations had cast doubt on that. Could she do it again? Did she even want to?

No. And it was time to stop pretending.

She looked over her shoulder, saw the worry for her in him, and her throat closed over. She shook her head as the tears pooled and fell.

"I'm not," she managed. "I'm not ok. I..." She sucked in a sobbing breath, trying to regain control enough to talk. "I thought I could tough it out; I thought I'd be fine on my own again but I'm afraid. I jump every time I hear a noise. I wake up screaming," she shuddered and wrapped her arms around herself, "feeling his hands on me. I can't help but think - what about his family? Will I spend the rest of my life looking over my shoulder for them?"

"Oh God, Kali, no!" Alex's voice was rough. "I thought Caz would've kept you in the loop. Max's family, his business partners, pretty much the whole organisation is in chaos. Most of them have been arrested and won't be getting out in a hurry, no matter how much they pay their lawyers. None of them know about your part or even your existence. You're safe."

He held out his arms and, after a moment's hesitation, she walked into them. He enfolded her. She relaxed her guard for the first time in years, and cried.

At last, he shifted and picked up a box of tissues she kept on the fridge. She accepted with a watery chuckle.

"I don't know what's wrong with me," she complained, embarrassed by her outburst. "I'm not usually this weepy. Don't encourage me to lean on you. Besides, you look exhausted. Did you sleep?"

He led her over to sit on the couch. "Not much the last few days. I've spent most of the last two days pouring out my life story to Caz's people and the Feds, and the night I brought you home you were pretty restless."

"So why didn't you leave and go get some sleep at home?" She blew her nose and wiped away the salt of past torments.

He cocked his head at her. "To be honest, I couldn't. You were crying in your sleep. I couldn't leave you alone like that."

She groaned, embarrassed all over again. "Oh, man. How pathetic. I'm sorry, Alex. Look, why don't you go get some sleep now. I'll be fine."

Alex leaned forward and took her hands in his. "Kali, you're a long way from fine and, in all honesty, so am I. But, for the first time in five years, I think I'm in a position where I can actually move on with life. What about you?"

She looked away, down at her hands, small in his. "I don't know, Alex. The last week, yesterday... it's all a lot to process. I don't...I don't really know where we stand. I still feel like you used me, even though I can see the position you were in, logically. It'll take me awhile to…trust you I guess." She studied him through her lashes. "The whole time I've known you, you always seemed so...distant; like you were angry and just barely keeping a lid on it. Where did this 'us' thing you say you want come from?"

He dropped her hands and let out a crack of laughter. He raised her chin with a finger, making her meet his eyes. They were soft with wry disbelief.

"For a smart, observant, astute girl, you're astonishingly blind," he said, leaning in to kiss her swiftly. "I've wanted to meet you since I first saw your photo on Caz's desk. You were leaning your head on his shoulder, smiling at the camera but you seemed sad. Then I got so focussed on Max, and so afraid you would tar me with the same brush as Rick, that I wasn't prepared to risk meeting you."

"But you-"

Another kiss shut her up.

"What you took as anger," he said, cupping her jaw gently, his expression both amused and bemused, "was nothing more than sheer frustration and hard-fought restraint. You were understandably wary of me, but I've known you, through Caz, for years. It wasn't until I actually met you, that I realised how absolutely incredible, sublimely beautiful, brilliant, strong and talented you really are; how badly Rick hurt you; how much my equal you are and how long I'd been searching for that... how much time I'd wasted."

"But I-" she tried again.

"Kali," he laid a thumb on her lips, shaking his head, "shut up and let me finish, please?"

She nodded.

"The minute I met you, defensive and ridiculous in that cowgirl outfit, I wanted you." He grimaced. "That sounds so damned trite but it's true. Then, the more I got to know you, the more you relaxed and let me in, the more insignificant going after Max seemed. When you disappeared after we made love," a shadow crossed his face, "I thought I'd blown it. I thought you were going to run and I'd never see you again."

"Oh," she whispered, shaking her head, "I'm sorry. I just didn't know how to handle it. I didn't know what to say. It was so much more amazing than anything. I got scared."

He smiled crookedly. "I figured as much. The whole time I was with you was an exercise in extreme restraint, believe me. Even now," his gaze dropped to her mouth, "you have no damned idea how much I want you; how much I want to hold you; make love to you; listen to you; have you lean on me; take care of you; stand by you." He stood up, shoving his hands deep in his pockets.

"Then you went and arranged the meeting with Max. I agreed to it because Caz's people insisted. They weren't going to let me go back to the island until I told you to go ahead. They kept Caz out of the meeting. Called it a 'conflict of interest'. So he didn't even know I'd come to see him; or about your text. Then his boss escorted me to the damned airport and watched me like a hawk. I couldn't call you. To top it all off I had plane trouble and my takeoff was delayed-"

"Plane trouble!" She grabbed at the couch arm, her stomach roiling at the image of his plane crashing into the sea.

Alex snorted. "Yes, and not accidental, either. Max'd hired someone to tamper with it. Luckily my ground crew found it before I took off."

He paced a few steps away, then came back. "I was going to stop you the minute I got back in phone range, but I couldn't get back in time." He glared at her and she flinched.

"But I thought the meeting with Max was what you wanted?" she murmured, bemused.

He laughed harshly. "For five wasted years yes, it was. Then I met you and suddenly it wasn't. The only reason I was going to go through with it at all was for you - to keep you and Amy safe and maybe to give Castor a shot at something with her. Once I'd met you, Max just didn't seem that important anymore." He paced around the room again, revealing some of the inner agitation she had sensed in him; a need, similar to her own, to be doing rather than sitting around.

"I pushed that plane to the limit to get back but you were already at the marina so I had to carry on with the plan. Lacey and I barely got out. Max's men were waiting for us. Then all I could do was search for the damned boat. I've never felt so helpless." He gave a bleak chuckle. "And so angry at you.

"The Coast Guard were tied up with a search and rescue of their own and by the time they were free you'd escaped and contacted Castor. My God," he sat back down again, admiration and fear warring on his handsome face, "I was never more proud and never more relieved in my whole life. You and Amy swam four kilometres that night. And then you were prepared to go back; to confront him again and risk your life. That blew me away. Why did you do that?"

Kali fiddled with a strand of hair, taken by surprise by the question. "I... it was important to you. I knew I could fix things for you, and I wanted to keep Amy safe too. Besides," she twisted her mouth in self-derision, "I was afraid of him and I told you, I don't like being afraid."

Alex smiled in soft wonder. "One of the many things I love about you."

He sat back down and picked up her hands, inspecting her wrists. The marks left by the cuffs were just a faint bruise. He kissed them, one at a time. She shivered at the touch of his lips on her skin.

"I read your report of what happened on the boat before I got there. You were... incredible." He regarded her with slumberous eyes. "With your permission," he ran his hands lightly up the soft inner skin of her arms until he held her face again, "I'd like to spend some time finding out exactly how incredible you are and repaying you for what you did for me."

She grabbed his wrists, troubled. "You don't owe me anything, Alex. I know what I said before, but it wasn't true. I went into the whole thing eyes open. Starting...something on the basis of repaying a debt isn't a great way to begin."

"Kali," he laughed, "I wasn't being literal. It was a metaphor."

"For wh...oh." She blushed.

He groaned. "Enough. Don't torture me any longer. Tell me if we have a chance."

She looked up again, half-tempted, half-afraid. Afraid of what? Afraid of opening up in case she got hurt again? Or afraid of the power he might exercise over her?

But hadn't she just said she didn't like being afraid? And Alex wasn't an insecure little boy, like Rick. He wasn't perfect, he had issues of his own, but who didn't? He only had power if she let him; if she didn't like herself enough and looked to others for approval. Hadn't she vowed to learn to be a better person? To be less afraid?

He watched her, open, vulnerable, clearly as afraid as she was.

She spread her hands wide and gave a mock-resigned shrug. "Well, I suppose you did buy me for a ten-day and today's the last day." She shifted on the couch and swung a leg over him so she sat astride his lap. "I'm all yours. Best get some value for money. Do what you want."

He gave a shout of laughter and shoved off the couch, wrapping an arm around her waist and hoisting her up as he stood. She hooked heels behind his back and fingers behind his neck.

He reached the bedroom and lowered them both gently onto the bed, never taking his eyes off hers. His face was alight with the same joy she'd seen briefly on the island; the wicked delight he'd hidden and half-forgotten.

"What I want, is to make sure you're never afraid again; to make sure you are thoroughly loved and happy; to make sure you know exactly how much I love you, every day."

Kali smiled up at him, running her hands over the bunched muscles of his shoulders and arms. "I'd like that. I love you too, Alex. That scares the hell out of me so I think I'll need a lot of practice at it before I'm not afraid any more. How does that sound?"

"Perfect." His grey eyes sparkled with humour. "And remember how you told me Kali is the goddess of death and destruction?"

She nodded.

His smile softened. "Did you know she also represents not only our fears, but the freedom we gain by facing them?"

She laughed softly. "I do now."

His face alight with amusement, awe and desire, he leaned down and kissed her with an expertise that took her breath away.

THE END

Discover other titles by Aiki Flinthart at:
www.aikiflinthart.com

The 80AD series
(YA Adventure/Fantasy)

80AD Book 1: *The Jewel of Asgard*
80AD Book 2: *The Hammer of Thor*
80AD Book 3: *The Tekhen of Anuket*
80AD Book 4: *The Sudarshana*
80AD Book 5: *The Yu Dragon*

The Kalima Chronicles
(YA Adventure/Fantasy)

IRON (Book 1)

ABOUT THE AUTHOR

Aiki Flinthart lives in Australia. In between running a business and being with her husband of many years, she pursues writing, archery, knife-throwing, martial arts, art, music, bellydancing and watches too much television. After many years of writing for her own amusement, she finally decided to write for others' – and discovered it was even more fun.

Discover other titles by Aiki Flinthart at:
www.aikiflinthart.com

Connect with Aiki on Facebook